Praise for *The Reader*

'*The Reader* is a fine novel, as far above a Holocaust genre as *Crime and Punishment* is above the average thriller. A sensitive, daring, deeply moving book about the tragic results of fear and the redemptive power of understanding' Ruth Rendell

'Crammed with incident and analysis, and yet Schlink finds room for virtuoso passages of evocation . . . compelling'
London Review of Books

'Until I read this novel I was not convinced that there was room for many more books about the Holocaust . . . the universal appeal of his sparely told story will remain' *Sunday Telegraph*

'He has thought so long and hard about German guilt that *The Reader* distils its questions, its answers, and its pure pain more simply and disturbingly than anything I've ever read' *The Spectator*

'Book reviewing can be a somewhat bleak trade . . . The infrequent bonus is the arrival, almost unheralded, of a masterly work. Then, the reviewer's sole and privileged function is to say as loudly as he is able "Read this" and "read it again"' George Steiner, *Observer*

'Achieves enormous moral force in the strength of its uncertainty . . . haunting and unforgettable' *Literary Review*

'Bernhard Schlink's extraordinary novel *The Reader* is a compelling meditation on the connections between Germany's past and present, dramatized with extreme emotional intelligence as the story of a relationship between the narrator and an older woman. It has won deserved praise across Europe for the tact and power with which it handles its material, both erotic and philosophical'
*Independent* Saturday Magazine

Bernhard Schlink was born in Germany in 1944. A professor of law at Humboldt University, Berlin, and Cardozo Law School, New York, he is the author of the major international bestselling novel *The Reader*, which was made into an Academy Award-winning film starring Kate Winslet and Ralph Fiennes. His works include the short-story collections *Flights of Love* and *Summer Lies* as well as several prize-winning crime novels. He lives in Berlin and New York.

# THE WOMAN ON THE STAIRS

Bernhard Schlink

Translated from the German
by Joyce Hackett and
Bradley Schmidt

WEIDENFELD & NICOLSON

A W&N PAPERBACK

First published in Great Britain in 2016
by Weidenfeld & Nicolson
This paperback edition published in 2017
by Weidenfeld & Nicolson
an imprint of the Orion Publishing Group Ltd
Carmelite House, 50 Victoria Embankment
London EC4Y 0DZ
An Hachette UK Company

1 3 5 7 9 10 8 6 4 2

A CIP catalogue record for this book is
available from the British Library.

ISBN (Mass Market Paperback) 978 1 4746 0100 9
ISBN (eBook) 978 1 4746 0066 8

Printed in Great Britain by Clays Ltd, St Ives plc

MIX
Paper from
responsible sources
FSC  FSC® C104740
www.fsc.org

www.orionbooks.co.uk

# Part One

# 1

Perhaps you will see the painting one day. Long lost, suddenly resurfaced – all the museums will want to display it. By now, Karl Schwind is one of the most famous and expensive painters in the world. When he turned seventy, I saw him in every paper, on every channel. Still, I had to look a long time before I recognized the young man in the old.

The painting, I recognized immediately. I walked into the last court of the Art Gallery and there it hung. It moved me as it had when I entered the parlour of Gundlach's villa, and saw it for the first time.

A woman descends a staircase. The right foot lands on the lower tread, the left grazes the upper, but is on the verge of its next step. The woman is naked, her body pale; her hair is blonde, above and below; the crown of her head gleams with light. Nude, pale and blonde – against a gray-green backdrop of blurred stairs and walls, the woman moves lightly, as if floating, towards the viewer. And yet her long legs, ample hips, and full breasts give her a sensual weight.

I approached the painting slowly. I felt awkward, just as I had back then. Then, it was because the woman who, a day before, had sat in my office in jeans, blouse, and jacket, approached me in the painting naked. Now I felt awkward because the painting brought up what happened back then, what I'd gotten myself into, and what I had soon banished from memory.

*Woman on Staircase*, the label read. The painting was on loan. I found the curator and asked him who had lent the painting. He said he couldn't disclose the name. I told him I knew the woman in the painting, and the owner of the painting, and that its ownership would likely be contested. He furrowed his brow, but again said he couldn't tell me the name.

# 2

My flight back to Frankfurt was booked for Thursday afternoon. Since the negotiations in Sydney finished up on Wednesday morning, I could have rescheduled for Wednesday afternoon. But I wanted to spend the rest of the day in the Botanic Garden.

I wanted to eat lunch there, lie on the grass, then see *Carmen* at the Opera House. I like the Botanic Garden, its Art Gallery, its Conservatory, the way it is bordered by a cathedral on the north, the Opera House on the south – its hills with their view onto the bay. It has a palm garden, a herb garden, and a rose garden; ponds, arbours, statues; many lawns with huge trees; grandparents with grandchildren; lonely men and women with their dogs; picnickers, lovers, people reading, people napping. On the veranda of the restaurant in the middle of the Garden, time stands still: old iron columns, an old cast-iron railing, trees filled with fruit bats, a fountain full of colourful birds with long, curved beaks.

I ordered food, and called my colleague. He had handled the Australian side of the merger, I, the German. We were, as is the case with mergers, partners as well as opponents. But we liked each other: we were the same age, both widowers, both senior partners at one of the last law firms that hadn't been taken over by the Americans or the English. I asked him which detective agency his firm used and he gave me the name.

"Is there a problem we can help with?"

"No, just something I've always been curious about."

I reached the head of the agency, and asked him to track down who owned the Karl Schwind in the Art Gallery of New South Wales, whether it was Irene Gundlach, or an Irene formerly Gundlach, and if a woman by that name lived in Australia. He said it could take a couple of days. I offered a bonus if he could tell me by the next morning. He laughed. Either he'd be able to obtain the information today at the Art Gallery, or it would take a couple of days, bonus or no bonus. He'd get back to me.

Then the food came, and with the food I ordered a bottle of wine I didn't want to finish, but finished anyway. Occasionally the fruit bats awoke, and all at once whooshed out from the branches, flew around the trees, then returned to their branches, and wrapped themselves back in their wings. Once in a while one of the colourful birds at the fountain let out a cry. Or a child cried out, or a dog barked, or the sound of a group of Japanese tourists wafted up like the twitter of a swarm of birds. Sometimes I heard only the chirr of cicadas.

On the slope below the Conservatory, I lay down on the grass. In my suit. Normally, the prospect of walking around in a wrinkled, even stained suit would have horrified me. Now it did not. I grew indifferent, too, to what awaited me in Germany. There was nothing I couldn't do without, nothing others couldn't do without me. In everything that lay before me, I was replaceable. I was irreplaceable only in what lay behind.

# 3

I hadn't actually wanted to become a lawyer. I had wanted
to be a judge. I had the necessary grades, I knew that judges
were in demand, and I was prepared to move wherever I
was needed. I regarded the interview at the Department of
Justice a formality. It was in the afternoon.

The head of personnel was an older man with kind eyes.
"You finished school at seventeen, passed your first state exam
at twenty-one and your second at twenty-three – I've never
seen an applicant so young, and rarely one so qualified."

I was proud of my grades and my youth, but wanted to
appear humble. "I was enrolled young, and the state changed
the school year twice, each time making us complete a year
in a semester."

He nodded. "A gift of two half-years. And you gained
another half-year when you didn't have to wait after the first
state exam, and became an apprentice right away. So you
have time to spare."

"I don't understand . . ."

"No?" He looked at me gently. "If you start next month,
you'll be judging others for forty-two years. You will sit on
high, they below; you will listen to them, talk to them, even
smile at them sometimes, but in the end you decide who's

in the right and who is wrong, who gets locked up and who goes free. Is that what you want – forty-two years up on the bench, forty-two years of being right? You think that will do you good?"

I didn't know what to say. In fact, I liked the prospect of sitting on high, dealing with others fairly, justly deciding their fates. Why not forty-two years?

He closed the file that lay before him. "Of course we'll take you if you really want. But I won't take you today. Come back next week, my successor can hire you. Or come back in a year and a half, when you've spent your extra time. Or in five years, when you've seen the world of law from below, as a lawyer, or a legal advisor, or a criminal investigator."

He stood up, and I stood up too, confused and at a loss for words. I watched him as he took his coat from the closet and lay it over his arm. Then I went with him out of the room, down the hall, down the stairs, and finally stood with him in front of the building.

"Do you feel the summer in the air? Not long now, and we'll have hot days, and balmy evenings, and warm rain-storms." He smiled. "God be with you."

I was annoyed. They didn't want me? Then I did not want them. I became a lawyer not to heed the old man's advice, but to spite it. I moved to Frankfurt, joined Karchinger and Kunze, a five-man firm, wrote a dissertation in my free time and made partner in three years. I was the youngest partner at any firm in Frankfurt, and was proud of it. Karchinger and Kunze were friends from their schooldays, and had gone to law school together. Kunze had no wife or children, Karchinger had a jovial wife from the Rhine Valley and a son my age, who was expected to join the firm one day. He struggled with his studies and I prepped him for his exams. Luckily, we got along well, and still do. Today he's a senior partner like me, and what he lacks in legal expertise, he makes up for in social finesse. He has landed important clients. That we now have seventeen junior partners and thirty-eight employees is his doing too.

# 4

For the first few years, I got the cases in which Karchinger and Kunze had no interest. A painter who had executed a commission, had been paid, and was now in dispute with the client – the seasoned manager of the firm gave me the case without even asking Karchinger or Kunze.

Karl Schwind did not come alone. He, in his early thirties, was accompanied by a woman in her early twenties. You would have taken them for strangers: with his tousled hair and overalls, he looked like a 1968 hippie, while her appearance was immaculate. She moved with poise, and sized me up coolly. When the painter became overwrought, she lay her hand on his arm.

"He doesn't want to let me take any pictures."

"You—"

"My portfolio was destroyed, so I have to take new pictures of some of the paintings. I know who bought them, I call these people, and they let me come and take pictures. They're happy to let me visit. He refuses."

"Why?"

"He doesn't say why. I called him, he hung up, and when I wrote him, he didn't reply." As he spoke, he threw up his hands, splayed open his fingers, clenched his fists, let them sink down. His hands were large, like everything else: his frame, his face, his eyes, his nose, his mouth. "I'm attached to my paintings. I can hardly stand to have to sell them."

I explained that the law gave artists the right to access their paintings for the purpose of making reproductions. "That is, if the artist has a legitimate interest and there is no conflicting legitimate interest on the part of the owner. Is there a reason that the owner might object?"

The painter stuck out his chin, pressed his lips together, and shook his head. I gave the woman a questioning look; she shrugged and smiled. He gave me the name of the painting's owner, Peter Gundlach, and his address, a prime location in the Taunus hills.

"How was your portfolio destroyed? Not that it matters, but if I can explain why—"

Once again he interrupted. I was annoyed with myself – back then I always got annoyed when I wasn't as assertive as I thought I should be. "I had an accident – my car went up in flames and so did the portfolio."

"I hope—"

"I was fine. But Irene was trapped inside and she," he placed his hand on her leg, "suffered burns."

"I'm so—"

He waved it away. "Nothing serious. Healed long ago."

# 5

I wrote to Gundlach, who wrote back immediately. He claimed he'd been misunderstood. Of course the painter could come by and take pictures of the painting. I relayed the response to Schwind and considered the matter resolved.

But a week later, Schwind was back. He was beside himself.

"Did he deny you access?"

"The painting is damaged. The right leg – it looks like he took a lighter to it."

"He?"

"Yes, Gundlach. He says it was an accident. But it wasn't an accident, it was intentional. I can tell."

"What do you want now?"

"What I want now?" The woman had come back with him, and again she placed her hand on his arm. But he still began to shout.

"What I want now? It's my painting. I had to sell it, and now it hangs on his wall, but it's my painting. I want to fix it."

"Did you offer to restore the painting?"

"He won't let me. Says he doesn't have a problem with a little mark, doesn't want me in his house, and he won't let the painting out of the house."

I found the story somewhat bizarre, but the two of them looked at me seriously, so I explained to them seriously that the legal situation was not a simple one. That, in the case of a damaged painting, the creator has the right to restore it only if the damage endangers his interests, that is, if a lot of people would see it. And that the owner of the painting, seen only in his private space, could do with it what he wanted. "I can write to Gundlach again with this or that legal argument. But if we have to go to court, it doesn't look good for us. What is the painting of, actually?"

"A woman descending a staircase." He looked around my office. "It's a big painting. You see that door? The picture's a little bigger."

"And who is the woman?"

"She's . . ." His tone became defiant. "She was Gundlach's wife."

# 6

Again Gundlach replied immediately. He regretted this new misunderstanding. Of course he was fine with letting the painter do the restoration. What could be better than having the artist himself restore the damaged artwork? He couldn't let the painting leave the house, or his insurance wouldn't cover it, but the painter could come to his house whenever he pleased. Again, I forwarded the response.

My curiosity was piqued. I went into a bookshop, and asked for everything they had on Karl Schwind. A few years before, the Frankfurt Art Association had organized an exhibition and published a slim catalogue – that was all they had. I know nothing about art and couldn't judge if the paintings were good or bad. There were pictures of waves, of skies and clouds, of trees; the colours were beautiful, and everything was blurry, the way I see the world when I'm not wearing my glasses. Familiar, yet distanced. The catalogue listed the galleries that had exhibited Schwind and the awards he had won. He didn't appear to be a failure as an artist, but he wasn't established either – up-and-coming, perhaps. He gazed at me from the back cover of the catalogue, too big for the suit he wore, too big for the chair he sat on, too big for the back cover.

Less than a week later, he was back in my office, again with the woman. He really was big, bigger than I had realized during his first visit. I am six foot two, slim, and have always been in good shape, and he was no taller than me, but so strong and angular that, next to him, I felt almost small.

"He did it again."

I had an idea of what had happened, but I never put words in my clients' mouths. "What did he do?"

"Gundlach damaged the painting again. I worked for two days on the leg, and when I went to finish it on the third day, there was an acid stain on the left breast. The paint is streaked, swollen, blistered – I need to scrape it off, re-prime it, and repaint it."

"What did he say?"

"That it must have been me. He said he'd found a little bottle among my things, and that the liquid smelled just like the stain. He insists that the painting be restored, at my expense, but not by me. He'll never trust me again." He looked at me, distraught. "What should I do? I won't let someone else near my painting."

"Are you ready to restore the new mark?" I was less and less sure what to make of the whole thing.

"Mark? It's not a mark. It's the left breast!" He reached for the left breast of the woman sitting next to him.

I was irritated, but she laughed – not embarrassed, not shy, but cheerful, her mouth a little crooked, a dimple in her cheek. She was blonde and I would have expected a light laugh. But her laugh was dark and smoky, and so was her voice. She said "Karl," and she said it affectionately, as if to an overeager, clumsy child.

"I offered to fix the painting again. I even offered to buy it back, even for double the price. But he wants none of it. He doesn't want to see me again."

This time I called Gundlach. He was friendly and contrite. "I don't know how he could have let this happen. But it goes without saying that it's as painful for him as it is for me, and that he wants to see the painting restored to its former beauty as much as I do. And no one can do that better than he. I neither accused him nor did I withdraw my trust. He's particularly sensitive." He laughed. "At least compared to people like you and me. Maybe for an artist, he's normal."

Schwind was both relieved and despondent. "Hopefully, it will all go well."

For three weeks I heard nothing from him. For three weeks he painted a new left breast. When he came to apply the finishing touches, he found the picture overturned – it had fallen over in the night, struck the small iron table he had set his paint and brushes on, and had been torn.

Gundlach called me. He was beside himself. "First the acid, now this – he may be a great artist, but he's horrendously careless. I can't force him to restore the picture yet again. But I have some influence, and I will make sure that he doesn't get another commission until he restores the picture."

The threat was unnecessary. Schwind, who came into the

agency that same day, was prepared to fix the picture, even if it would cost him another few weeks. But he was desperate. "What if he does it again?"

"You mean . . ."

"Oh, I know that it was him. You think a painter can't lean a picture against a wall so that it stays? No, he knocked it over, and he made that tear with a knife. The table's edge is too dull to make such a sharp cut in the canvas." He laughed bitterly. "You know where the tear is? Here." This time he ran his hand not over the woman, but over his own belly and crotch.

"Why would he do that?"

"Out of hate. He hates the picture, because it's of his wife, and he hates his wife because she left him. And he hates me."

"Why should he . . ."

"He hates you because I left him for you." She shook her head. "He doesn't hate the picture. He doesn't care about it in the slightest. He wants to get at you and he gets at you when he damages the painting."

"Instead of having it out with me, he destroys the picture? What kind of man is that?" Schwind couldn't contain his outrage and contempt, and leapt to his feet. Then he sat back down, and let his shoulders droop.

I tried to make sense of what I had heard. She had modelled for the painter and run off with him? Traded in the old man for the young one? Squeezed as much out of the old man in the divorce as she could squeeze?

But she wasn't my client, he was. "Forget about him and the picture. Legally he can't touch you, and I wouldn't take his threat to use his influence seriously. Write the picture off, however much it hurts. Or paint it again. I hope, to an artist, that's not an offensive suggestion."

"It is not. But I can't write off the picture. And maybe . . ." He sat there, quietly. His face changed, and all its despair, contempt and outrage fell away; it became childlike, and the big man with the big face and big hands looked at us trustingly. "You know, maybe the damage to the leg really was an accident. When Gundlach saw it, he didn't like the damaged painting any more. Then he thought that the damage kept his memories at bay, and that his life was easier without those memories. That's why he defaced the painting again. But when he sees it restored to its original beauty, he loves it again."

"I don't get the impression that Gundlach's a man who can be seduced by art." I looked at her questioningly, but she said nothing — didn't nod, didn't shake her head, only looked lovingly at Schwind, as if bemused and enchanted by his childlike nature. I tried again. "You're playing into his hands. He can deface the painting again and again. You will never be able to do your own work."

He looked at me sadly. "In the last six months I haven't finished a single painting."

# 8

He'd estimated it would take a month or two to restore the picture, and I was sure I would see him back in my office afterwards. But summer went by and he didn't come. In October I had an important case, and thought no more about him.

But one morning the firm's manager announced the arrival of Irene Gundlach. She came wearing a jacket, blouse, and jeans, and at first I thought she was underdressed for the autumn day, but then I looked out the window. The morning clouds had passed, the sky was blue, and the sun had lit the leaves of the chestnut tree with a golden glow.

She gave me her hand and sat down. "I'm coming on Karl's behalf. He would thank you personally, but he's in a phase of utter concentration. Gundlach was in the US for the last few months and left him alone. Karl didn't just restore my picture, he also started a new one." She laughed. "You wouldn't recognize him. Now that the burden of my painting has been lifted from his shoulders, he's a whole new man."

"That's good to hear."

She did not stand up, but crossed her legs instead. "Please send the bill to me, Karl doesn't have money, he'd have to give it to me anyway." She saw the question in my eyes, even before I had thought it. "It's not Gundlach's money. It's mine." She smiled. "How must our story seem to you? A rich old man has his young wife painted by a young artist, they fall in love and run away. It's a cliché, isn't it?" She smiled again. "We love clichés because there's truth to them. Although . . . is Gundlach already an old man? Is Karl still a young painter?" She laughed, and again I was surprised by the dark laughter of the blonde woman with the pale skin and the bright gaze. She squinted as she laughed. "Sometimes I wonder if I'm still a young woman."

I laughed with her. "Well what else?"

She grew serious. "When you're young, you have the feeling that everything can still turn out for the best – everything that's gone wrong, everything you've missed out on, everything that you've broken. Once you lose that feeling, once things are beyond repair, you're old. I no longer have that feeling."

"Then I was never young. My mother died when I was four – how could anything have made that right? My grandmother didn't bring my mother back."

She trained her bright gaze on me. "You've never been in love, have you? Maybe you'll have to get older to become young. To find everything in a woman, to find it all again: the mother you lost, the sisters you missed out on, the daughter you dream of." She smiled. "We're all those things when we are truly loved." She stood up. "Will we see each other again? I hope not – don't misunderstand me, please don't. If we do see each other again, that will mean everything's come apart. Do you ever wonder whether God envies our happiness, and has to destroy it?"

# 9

I wanted to dismiss her and her talk. Whether Gundlach's or her own, she seemed to have enough money, and no need to work: an idler. But she wouldn't be dismissed. She sat in my mind with her crossed legs, tight jeans, tight blouse, her bright gaze and dark laugh – relaxed, defiant, confusing. I was confused enough while we sat across from each other, and even more so the next day, when I went to Gundlach's house and saw the painting.

No, I thought, as Gundlach approached and greeted me. This is not an old man. He could have been forty; he was slender, had a full head of black hair and graying temples, and he moved and spoke with vigour. "Thank you for coming. Your client and I don't get on well. I'm sure you and I will do better."

Had it been up to me, I wouldn't have driven up to the Taunus to visit Gundlach. I would have insisted that he, who wanted something from me, come to me. But Gundlach had called the firm's manager and the firm's manager had promised a visit. "Refuse to visit Gundlach? You still have a lot to learn." He told me about Gundlach's business, fortune, and connections. So I drove there, was let in by the butler, and had to wait in the foyer like a supplicant.

That Gundlach took me by the arm was another blow to my pride. He led me into the drawing room. To the right, a row of windows with a view over the plain; to the left, a wall of books; straight ahead, on a white wall, the picture. I stopped in my tracks, I had to, and Gundlach let go of my arm. You've never been in love . . . when we're truly loved . . . the happiness God envies – all that she'd said the day before, she now promised as she walked down the staircase naked.

"Yes," Gundlach said. "A beautiful painting. But it's as if it's cursed. Leg, breast, crotch – it's one thing after another." He shook his head. "Is the damage over with? I wonder. What about you?"

"I—"

"What if it goes on? Should Schwind keep coming back, again and again? I don't want him in the house any more, and he'd rather paint new pictures than restore old ones. But he has to, he has no choice. And I have to let him into the house to restore it, because the law demands it. Isn't that how it is?"

He looked at me, his eyes friendly but mocking. He had his lawyers, and knew that Schwind's legal position was weak. But he also knew that I had to act as if it were strong. I could not betray my client. I could not tell Gundlach that he was playing a vile game. I nodded.

"Schwind would like the picture back. He feels that, as long as the picture is at my place, it won't come to rest – and nor will he. Wouldn't you agree that everything has a place where it belongs? If it isn't where it belongs, it won't come to rest. Paintings don't come to rest, and neither do people."

23

"If rest is a concern – not just for my client but for you as well – he'll gladly buy the painting back."

"He said as much to me. But it isn't just about the painting. You see how she descends the stairs? Collected, relaxed, peaceful? When she came to the bottom, her peace was done with. Because it's a place she doesn't belong."

"Your wife doesn't give me the impression—"

"Don't interrupt me!" He needed a moment to recover from his agitation at my impertinence. "Impressions can be deceiving. Doesn't the painting make a good impression, though it's cursed? What matters is not the impression that my wife makes, but that she's lost her peace. And that she finds it again."

I waited to see if he would continue. But he stood there and looked at the painting. "I don't understand."

He turned to me. "Schwind comes tomorrow. I'm supposed to give the restored painting my approval, as it were. If something happens to the painting before tomorrow, if Schwind then comes to you, if he comes without my wife, if he asks you to prepare a strange contract – do it. Even if you find it unsettling, it's the right thing. Don't we live in strange times? And contracts can be important, even if they can't be enforced in court."

I didn't understand him, but didn't want to say again that I didn't understand him. He looked at me, laughed, took my arm again and led me back to the foyer. "Don't take this personally, but lawyers tend to lack imagination. When I meet one who takes on challenges, I take note."

# 10

On the drive home I knew I had fallen in love with Irene Gundlach.

I knew it though I had no experience in love. I'd liked our mathematics teacher, a small woman with lively eyes, a clear voice, and short skirts. Once I secretly stuck a red rose in the clamp on her bicycle rack. Then there was a classmate I couldn't take my eyes off. Wherever I was in town, I hoped I would run into her, would talk to her – something I dared not do in school – and she would happily respond. Sometimes, day after day, I could think of nothing but her, what she might be doing, what I could do to be noticed and liked by her, and how it would be to be together. But when a difficult test loomed, for which I had to thoroughly prepare, I decided I would think no more about her until after the test. After that I thought of her no more. At law school, there were hardly any women students, and I did not meet women from other departments. Between semesters, I earned money for my studies working in a spare parts warehouse where, besides the forklift operators, and the other students, only women worked. They cracked lewd jokes about us men, and made obscene advances that left me embarrassed, and helpless about how to react. One of the women, I liked, quieter than the others, young, with dark hair and soulful eyes, and on my last day I waited for her at the warehouse gate. When she came out, she went straight across the street towards a young man who was leaning against a tree.

Maybe you get it, about women and love, if you have a mother and sisters. When my mother died, my father gave me to his parents, who might have liked to spoil me, the way grandparents like to spoil grandchildren, but didn't feel like raising me. This duty, they had fulfilled with their own four children, and they found no joy in repeating the experience; with me, they got through it as efficiently and matter-of-factly as possible. Not that I lacked anything. I had piano and tennis lessons, went to dance classes, learned to drive. But that was as far as it went; beyond that, my grandparents let me know that they preferred to be left alone.

Here is how I'd imagined falling in love: I'd get to know a woman, we'd like each other, meet up, like each other more and more, meet up again and again, grow ever closer, then finally fall in love. And that's how it went, a couple of years later, with my wife. She started at the firm as an apprentice, she was dedicated and cheerful, and she accepted my invitations to meals, the opera, and museums, first once a week, then more frequently. We grew ever closer and married after she passed her second state exam. Once the children were older she went into local politics and became a city councilwoman. Just after her re-election, she had a car accident. It's ten years since she died, and to this day, I do not understand how, in early afternoon, she could have had a blood alcohol concentration of .16, and driven off a country road into a tree. Had she been an alcoholic? the police had asked. My wife, an alcoholic?

The force with which my desire for Irene Gundlach over-
came me – nothing had prepared me for it, and luckily, it
never happened again. On the drive back to Frankfurt I had
to stop and get out of the car because I was so dazed. So it
existed – a happiness I wouldn't have dreamed of, and all
it took was this one woman, her closeness, her voice, her
nakedness. She hadn't taken the last step from the staircase
of her old life into a new life – if only she would take it into
mine, and if, every morning, she would step into my arms!

# 11

By Wednesday evening, the head of the detective agency hadn't called, so I called him Thursday morning. I couldn't reach anybody. Only after ten did I get a secretary, who connected me to his cell phone. I'd thought a good detective agency would be staffed round the clock, or at least from early morning.

"I told you it could take a couple days."

"I have to go back to Germany today."

"I have your telephone number. Can you give me your email address? I'll let you know as soon as I have something."

"And then I'm supposed to fly back here?"

He laughed. "That's up to you."

It was an easy laugh, and I pictured an older gentleman with a belly and bald head. Was I supposed to fly back — what a foolish question. I gave him my email address and hung up. Then I stood at the window and looked at the harbour, the Opera House with its billowing concrete sails, the blue bay with ships large and small and, at the end of the bay, the green strip of land, behind which lay the open sea. The sun was shining. I could skip breakfast, eat lunch early at the restaurant in the Botanic Garden, and then lie down in the grass again. I could buy a backpack at the leather and luggage place I had passed near the hotel, a book from the bookstore, a bottle of red from the wine shop, and read, and drink, and fall asleep, and wake up.

I thought about the flight I was supposed to take that afternoon, about arriving the next morning, the drive home, unlocking the door, unpacking, showering, going through the post in my dressing gown, shaving and dressing, driving to the office, and being welcomed back. I thought of the words I'd exchange with the driver: he would ask me if I had had a pleasant journey; I would ask him whether anything had happened in Frankfurt. I thought of the flowers my secretary would place on my desk.

I thought about the ritual of homecoming, and it made me sad. I had adhered to it all these years, and the years themselves had become a ritual faithfully adhered to, case by case, client by client, contract by contract. Mergers and acquisitions – that was what I was good at, what clients came to me for, and what the contracts were about. Over the years I had learned the points to be considered, the questions to be asked. I always considered the same points, always asked the same questions. There were only problems when the other side tried some ruse. But I, too, had my ruses.

I called the head of my travel agency in Frankfurt. It was far too late to reach him at the office, but I reached him at home. He said he could rebook my flight, but only to a specific date. When would I want to fly? I didn't know yet? Then he would simply move it by two weeks, and he could move it forwards or backwards, at any time. He wished me a pleasant stay.

I put on the suit I had worn the day before, wrinkled and stained by dirt and grass. Suddenly my decision not to

fly home frightened me. Suddenly the rituals I followed –
at work, in leaving and returning home, in my free time
– seemed to be the only thing holding my life together.
How would I live without them? But I did not reverse the
postponement of my flight.

# 12

I couldn't spend the day at the Botanic Garden without going to the Art Gallery. Once again I stood before the painting, and once again the woman made me feel awkward. Not because she was naked, and not because she reminded me of what had happened in the past. Rather, because the woman I saw wasn't the one I'd encountered back then, the woman I had seen until now. Why hadn't I seen it before?

The woman in the picture was not descending the staircase to play the piano, or to drink tea, or because her lover was happily waiting at the bottom. She was descending the staircase with bowed head and downcast eyes, as if under duress, but duress she had submitted to. As if she had resisted, but had given up because whoever controlled her was too powerful. As if she could only plead for clemency with softness, seduction, and surrender. Risking, simply to be taken. Or was that what she wanted? Without admitting it to her master, or even to herself?

In a museum I had once seen nineteenth-century paintings of white slave girls in Arabic or Turkish harems. Columns, marble, cushions, fans, the women naked, in lascivious poses, with inscrutable eyes. Kitsch, I had thought. Was the woman descending the staircase and coming towards me kitsch as well? I didn't know. The jumble of power and seduction, resistance and surrender felt awkward. It was not a terrain I had ever encountered women on. It did not fit with how I had experienced Irene Gundlach back then. Or had I gotten it all wrong?

I did not want to think about it. Luckily, I had the book and the red wine. I don't read novels, but books about history. What really happened – that is something different from what somebody makes up. When we learn from history, we learn from reality, not from sometimes inspired, but often ridiculous fantasies. And people who find novels more colourful than history are not taxing their imagination: they are not picturing Caesar, who loves Brutus like a son, and gets stabbed to death by him; the Aztecs, who get decimated by the white man's diseases, even before they meet in battle; the women and children with Napoleon's army who, crossing the Berezina, get trampled in the snow, or pushed into the icy water. Tragedies and comedies, good and bad luck, love and hate, joy and grief – history offers it all. Novels can't offer more.

I read about the history of Australia, the convicts in chains, the settlers, the land grant companies, the gold miners, the Chinese. The Aborigines who died first from infections, then from being massacred, and then had their children taken away. The taking was well intentioned, it brought tremendous suffering to both parents and children. My wife would have nodded; she liked to say that the opposite of good is not evil, but good intentions. But the opposite of evil is not evil intentions, but good.

# 13

As Gundlach had predicted, Schwind turned up at the firm the next day. He came directly from Gundlach, and sat in the chair in front of my desk, head bowed, hands folded. He remained silent for so long that I became impatient. Even when he started to speak, he did not raise his head or unfold his hands.

"When I arrived, the painting hung on the wall. I showed Gundlach my work, and he saw and praised it. Then he took out a pocketknife, opened it, made a cut in the painting, closed the knife, put it back in his pocket. I could have stopped him; he did it all slowly and calmly. But it was as if I was paralyzed. Then he smiled and said: 'You'll fix this in no time.' He was right, the cut is small, and on the staircase. 'But you'll only find rest when you have the painting and I get back what's mine. Go to your lawyer and have him draw up a contract.' I asked: 'A contract?' He said: 'We have to make it right.'"

He raised his head and looked at me. "Can you do that? Draw up a contract so I get the picture back and he gets Irene?"

I said nothing, but he saw the horror on my face.

"I must get the picture back, I must. Do you think I'll let

Gundlach damage it again? Or let him destroy it? I should never have sold it to him. When Irene and I got involved, I should have given back the deposit and taken the painting with me. I was dumb, by God, was I dumb. I know now that I can only paint when I can decide what happens to the painting. Some paintings I've destroyed. Because they weren't right. This painting is right. One day it will hang in the Louvre, or the Met, or the Hermitage. You don't believe me? You're right, maybe I'll need the money and will be happy if I can sell the picture to Berlin, or Munich, or Cologne. But then a different painting of mine will hang in the Met. And one day I'll have a retrospective in New York, to which Berlin will lend the painting." He spoke with ever more agitation, throwing up his hands, splaying out his fingers, clenching his fists, then letting them sink down again. Suddenly he laughed. "Maybe I'll come to the opening of the exhibition and remember you when I see the painting." He laughed some more and shook his head.

Then he became upset again. "But the painting won't be sent to New York without my consent. Never again will I sell a painting without retaining the power to decide what happens to it, who buys it, who gets it on loan. You think buyers won't agree to that? Buyers will fight over my paintings and agree to everything I demand. You don't believe me. You can't believe that a little sketch that I scribble on your notepad would make you rich one day. You'd rather be paid by Irene. You take me for somebody who's not talented enough or persistent enough – or you think I'm too crotchety for the art market."

I wanted to object, but he wouldn't let me interrupt, and dismissed me with a wave. "If only he'd do something abstract, you're thinking – or at least something like Warhol. Soup cans or Coke bottles or Marilyn Monroe – that's what you like, admit it, that's what you like. Here in your office you have old engravings, at home you have Warhol's Goethe or Beethoven because you want to show that you're educated, but not old-fashioned, you're open to everything modern. Isn't that right?"

His tone was contemptuous, his gaze hostile. I wanted to explain what paintings hung in my apartment and why, but then I decided it was none of his business. He could think whatever he wanted. "Your painting is more important to you than your lover?"

"You have no idea what you're talking about. What do you know about my painting? What do you know about the woman? Nothing. Not about the painting, not about the woman. Maybe she wants to go back to her husband. To the comfort he offers: the servants, the holidays, the horses, the tennis, the money. Have you asked yourself that? What will she do when her money runs out and my paintings don't yet earn enough? Work as a waitress? As a cleaning lady? In a factory? And why should you care about any of this?"

"I'm supposed to draw up a contract. A perverse contract. And you ask why I should care?"

"Slow down. Irene Gundlach is a grown woman. It doesn't matter what you write, what her husband and I sign – she can do what she wants. If I tell her it's over, and if he tells her she belongs to him again, she can tell him to go to hell, and tell me she doesn't believe me. Don't talk to me about perverse. Two men have got into a mess and want to sort it out, and whether they succeed depends on the woman. An old story."

During the last few sentences he'd calmed down. He was brusque but in control of himself. He stood up. "I'll agree to whatever terms. Let him decide when and where and how what needs to happen happens. You know how to reach me."

# 14

Today, if a client came to me with such a request, I'd show him the door. Back then I didn't know what to say, and watched silently as Schwind left the room.

Should I speak to one of the two senior partners? But my reputation in the firm was partly built on never asking for help, but rather solving all problems myself. I thought of the first judge for whom I had worked as a clerk and with whom I had an especially close relationship. I could imagine what he would say.

The phone rang; the firm's manager had Gundlach on the line. Had Gundlach hired a detective to shadow Schwind and report when he entered and left my office?

"You're considering what you should put down in the contract. It's not for me to meddle in your work. But allow me to make a suggestion. It's best if Schwind and Irene come to me. We'll talk a little, then Schwind will take the painting to his car, and say he'll come back to pick up Irene – but he'll drive away with the painting instead. When I explain to Irene that Schwind has swapped her for the picture, she'll know to whom she belongs."

"What if she doesn't know?"

He laughed. "Let that be my concern. I know her. When

she left we were going through a bad patch, and she thought she'd find true love not with me but with him. After the swap, she'll know better." I said nothing. "Hello? You don't believe me? You're asking yourself what happens if she still doesn't get it? Don't worry, I won't put her in chains and lock her in the cellar. If she wants a taxi, she'll get a taxi." His tone became imperious. "So draw up the contract, have Schwind and me sign it, and set up the meeting." He hung up.

Put her in chains and lock her in the cellar? No, not like that. But what if he kidnapped her and took her somewhere? To his country house or his Aegean island? If he drugged her, and she woke up on his yacht or in his jet, and because she had no choice but to grin and bear it, she would write me a postcard, saying she was enjoying a second honeymoon with Gundlach?

I imagined the conversation, the struggle, and the drugging. Would Gundlach do it alone? Or would the butler hold her down while Gundlach pressed the chloroform-soaked rag to her face? Would they carry her to the car together? Would Gundlach himself drive? Then I imagined a different scenario. What if Schwind tricked Gundlach? If he told Irene everything? If she helped him get the picture back, then ran away with him? Gundlach would not tolerate that, he would have people hunt them down, punish Schwind and kidnap her. Or would he be so furious that he would have her not just kidnapped, but also punished? Beaten, raped, mutilated? No, Schwind had to know that he couldn't betray Gundlach. The exchange would take place.

# 15

Gundlach retired only a few years ago, passing the reins of the company to his daughter. He was a skilled businessman who had successfully expanded into Eastern Europe, America, and China, had advised Kohl and Schröder on the economics of German reunification. Had he wanted to, he could have become President of the Federation of German Industries. We occasionally crossed paths socially. His promise to keep me in mind, if I brought him and Schwind together, came to nothing.

Yes, I did the deal between Gundlach and Schwind, just as they wanted. I drew up the contract, setting out the exchange according to Gundlach's suggestion, and had both of them sign it. The exchange was scheduled for five o'clock on Sunday.

In addition, I resolved to warn Irene Gundlach. Should I summon her to the firm? Ask her to come alone? But what if Schwind accompanied her anyway? Or she found my request odd, and didn't come? I knew where she and Schwind lived, took a day off, and parked my car so that I had a view of the entrance to the old apartment building. I didn't have to wait long; at nine o'clock, she stepped out of the door and walked down the street. I followed her on the opposite side. We took the metro to the city centre, and in the rush of the exiting crowd, our encounter seemed coincidental enough.

"How nice to run into you. There's been a turn of events I wanted to talk to you about. Do you have a moment?"

Was she surprised? She seemed relaxed, and smiled. "I have to cross the river. Would you accompany me?"

We walked through the old city and over the bridge and along the park by the river, discussing the changing face of the city, the upcoming elections, the beautiful autumn. Morning fog still hung over the river, but the colourful leaves were already lit up by the sun. I reminded her that the sun had also been shining and the leaves glowing when she visited my office.

We sat down on a bench, and I told her about my visit to Gundlach, about Schwind's visit to my office, and the contract that I had drawn up and the two men had signed. I told her my fear for what Gundlach could do to her if she didn't co-operate. I did not know how she took my news. I did not look at her. I looked at the city across the river. As I spoke, I watched the fog thinning, drifting apart, dissolving. When I finished, the city was bathed in light.

When I finally looked at her, she had tears in her eyes, and I quickly looked away. "It's okay," she said with a voice that belied the tears. "Just a few tears." Then she asked: "Why the contract? What do they get out of it?"

"I think Gundlach wanted to give the agreement a binding formality, even though it can't legally be enforced. In olden days he would have challenged Schwind to a duel."

"And you? What do you get out of the contract?"

"If I hadn't drawn it up Gundlach would have found another lawyer. And I wouldn't have known what he and Schwind were planning for you."

"As a lawyer, are you allowed to do this? You represent one of my two men, then you're in cahoots with the other, then you tell me everything?"

"I don't care."

She nodded. "So on Sunday . . . No, my husband doesn't have a yacht or a jet, or an island. But he does have a country house. Is he capable of drugging and abducting me? I don't know."

"Your husband? Aren't you divorced?"

"He has his lawyers delaying the proceedings." She sounded irritated, and I did not know if the cause was my curiosity or Gundlach's resistance.

"I'm sorry."

"You don't have to constantly apologize."

I wanted to say that I did not constantly apologize. But then I let it be. I sat there and did not know how I should say what I wanted to say: that I wanted to help her, that I was ready to do anything, give up anything, for her. That I loved her.

"What have I got myself into with these two men of mine! One wants to sell me, the other maybe to abduct me." She laughed. "And you? What do you want?"

I blushed. "I . . . I was involved in getting you into this situation, and I'd like to do whatever I can to help you out of it. If I . . . if you . . ."

She looked at me – surprised? moved? with pity? I couldn't read her. Then she smiled, ran her hand over my head, neck and shoulders, and held me briefly. "I got mixed up with

41

the bad guys but I'm not lost. A brave knight has come to rescue me."

"Are you mocking me? I don't mean that I'm anything special. I'm . . . I love you."

# 16

I love you – I immediately sensed that this degree of intimacy did not sound right. You should probably keep your mouth shut if "I love you" does not sound right. But out of the abundance of the heart, the mouth speaks. Now I wanted to talk my way out of my stilted declaration into a better one, by laying out the love I felt.

"It happened when you came to the firm alone. You spoke of love, of what a woman who's really loved becomes – lover, mother, sister, daughter – of a joy so great that God would envy us. You smiled when you said it – a joyful, pained, wise smile that held a promise. You didn't promise me anything, there's nothing I want to hold you to, for God's sake, the promise was a . . . a cosmic promise, I know you were speaking of love, and women, *per se*. But for me, you are woman *per se*, and to love and be loved by you . . ."

"Shhh." She put her arm around my shoulders again and pulled me close. "Shhh." I stopped talking, hoping the embrace would never end, and closed my eyes. "If you really want to help me . . ."

"What?" I opened my eyes. "What?"

"You can . . ." She broke off, and took her arm away, and sat up straight. I also sat up straight.

Then she began to talk, at first haltingly, then with more certainty. "When we drive to Gundlach on Sunday . . . Karl won't want to drive my car, he'll want his VW bus. I can . . . I can give you my key, and when we've gone into Gundlach's house, you sneak into the van and hide behind the wheel. When Karl has brought the picture out of the house and put it in the van, and shut the door . . . Everything depends on you driving off immediately. That you leave right away. If Karl manages to open one of the doors and jump in, it's over. But if he doesn't, I'm sure Karl will think Gundlach betrayed him. He'll come back into the house, accuse Gundlach, and while the two of them fight, I can get away. Down below Gundlach's house, where the garden ends, there's a bend in the road. That's where you wait. I'll climb over the wall and get into the van with you."

I tried to react with the same sangfroid with which she had laid out her plan. "Will Schwind park so I don't have to turn around?"

She nodded. "I'll make sure of it. Don't worry about the gate either – it's only closed at night." She smiled at me. "If you drive off as soon as the door slams, and I run the minute my two men lock horns – we'll have pulled it off."

I didn't like her talking about her two men, but I said nothing. I pictured the slope of the land outside Gundlach's house, the driveway to the gate, the greenery, the parking place. Yes, I could probably sneak into the van. I did not know what would happen if things went wrong, I was crossing a line that I'd never crossed. But I was determined. "When you get into the van, where will we go?"

She ran her hand over my head again. "Where do you think?"

44

# 17

What could that mean, but that she'd be with me? I was happy. We belonged together. We would act together, succeed together, escape together. We did not even have to escape, we could stay put – what could we be accused of? I dreamed of our life together. Would we get a big apartment, or a small house? Did she garden, did she cook? What did she actually do all day? Did she like to travel, and where? Did she like reading, and what? Did she . . .

"I have to go." She tore me from my dream, and stood up.

I stood up too. "Can I accompany you?"

"It's just a short walk." She pointed to the Museum of Arts and Crafts.

"There?"

"I work there. Design."

Suddenly I was afraid. The beautiful woman, with whom I dreamed of a life, already had one. She had a job, she had earned or inherited money, she had been with men, Gundlach and Schwind weren't accidents, but decisions. "Design" – she said it short and clipped, as if she didn't want me to know more about her than necessary.

"When will you give me the key?"

"I'll drop it in your mailbox. Where do you live?"

I gave her my address. "You have to ring the bell. The mailboxes are in the main hallway. When will you come?"

"I don't know. If you're not there, then I'll just buzz until someone opens."

Then she was gone. She walked along the riverbank, crossed the street, and went into the museum. Crossing the street, as she looked left and right to check for traffic, she could have looked back at me and waved. But she didn't look back.

I sat back down on the bench. Should I go to the firm? I could still put in a day's work. I didn't want to. When, in the Botanic Garden, I remembered that morning by the river, it occurred to me that I had never done that again, fritter away a day. Of course, with my fiancée, then wife, and then with my children, there were days when I didn't work. But on those days I did what I owed my fiancée, my wife and children, what served our health, education, togetherness. Pleasant activities, certainly, and a nice change of pace from work. But just to sit, and watch the world go by, and close my eyes against the sun, and daydream hour after hour, to find a restaurant with good food and wine, take a little walk, then find another place to sit and watch, and close my eyes against the sun, and dream – I did that only that day, and now again in Sydney.

I wonder what I was dreaming of back then. Surely, of life with Irene. But surely not just that. Probably I pondered the past, as I do now. Since I seemed on the verge of finding happiness, maybe the past began to look different. Maybe I saw my childhood with my grandparents not as loveless, but as a path to freedom, saw my career not as a pressure to succeed, but as a gift of success; and saw, in my unfulfilled encounters with women, not failure but promise.

I do not rue my age. I don't envy the young for the lives they have ahead of them; I do not want mine before me again. But I do envy them their short past. When we're young, we can survey our past. We can give it meaning, even if that meaning constantly changes. Now, looking over the past, I have no idea what was a blessing, what a curse; whether my career was worth the price; and when my encounters with women succeeded, and when they failed.

# 18

I went to see the painting again on Friday. The Art Gallery was full of students and their teachers. I liked the sound of so many voices, talking and calling out to each other; it reminded me of break time in the schoolyard, of summer days at the pool. A couple of teenagers stood in front of the painting, critiquing the woman's figure. Were the hips too wide, the thighs too thick, the feet too small? I did not go up to them, but stood close enough that my presence bothered them, and they moved on.

I saw no flaw in the woman. But I didn't see her as I had last seen her. Yes, she was softness, seduction, and surrender. She no longer offered up resistance. And yet she had not really given up. The tilt of her head, her lowered eyes and shut mouth bespoke hidden resistance, refusal, spite. She would never belong to the one who had power over her. She would play along, but would remain elusive.

Could I have seen that already then, and known how things would end? I was only briefly in Gundlach's drawing room, and had had to listen to what he said, and couldn't really look at the picture. If I'd been able to take a closer look, would I have known then?

She didn't drop off the keys that evening. I took another

day off, wanting to be at home if she came. I went shopping early, and was anxious when I got back and looked in the mailbox. But she had not left the keys. I am orderly, even fastidious, and I didn't have to clean up my apartment for Irene. But I did put flowers in a vase, and fruit in a bowl. Because I was afraid that she might not like pedantic people, I let a couple of apples roll onto the table, scattered some books and periodicals on the floor next to the armchair, and spread out the draft of an article on my desk.

She came the next day. She rang the bell, and without looking out of the window, I knew it was her. Instead of buzzing her in, I ran down the stairs and opened the main door.

"I just wanted . . ." She held the key in her hand.

"Come up for a minute. We have to talk."

She went up the stairs ahead of me, with a quick step, and I took in her feet, her flat shoes, her bare calves, her thighs and bottom in tight pants that ended just below the knee. I had left my apartment door open, and she entered slowly, looking around, completely at ease. She walked into the large room that I used as a living room and work room, walked over to the window, looked down at the street, then looked over the manuscript on my desk. "What are you writing?"

"The Federal Supreme Court handed down a ruling on copyright law . . ." I could not continue. I hadn't taken her into my arms downstairs, and would have liked to do it now, but with my charmless smile, my too-long arms, my too-big hands, and my clunky movements, it seemed so wrong that I didn't dare.

"Copyright law . . . what do we need to discuss?"

"Don't you want to sit down? Would you like tea or coffee or . . ."

"Nothing, thank you, I need to be off." But she sat down in the armchair I had surrounded with books and periodicals, and I sat down in the one opposite.

"When I go to Gundlach's tomorrow . . . It's a wealthy neighbourhood. Will my car look out of place if I park on the street? Will I look out of place there? Do the people all know each other, and will they notice a stranger?"

"Leave your car in the village you have to drive through to get to Gundlach. From there you walk, it's half an hour, no more. Are you afraid?" She scrutinized my face.

I shook my head. "I'm glad. That you and I . . . What I said two days ago . . . I ambushed you. I'd like to say it again, this time better, but I'm afraid I'd ambush you again, and I'd rather wait until we have all the time in the world. No, I'm not afraid. You?"

She laughed. "That it won't work out? That I'll be reviled? That I'll be abducted?"

"I don't know. What will you do with the painting?"

"Nothing, as long as I don't have it." She stood up. "I have to go."

Where to? I'd have liked to ask, and whether she loved me back, or might one day, and whether she was still sleeping with Schwind, and how it would go on Sunday, when we were sitting in the car. I asked her none of that. I stood up and wrapped my arms around her. She did not nuzzle into me, but neither did she recoil, and when she stepped back, she kissed me on the cheek, and ran her hand over my head. "You're a good kid."

# 19

I really was not afraid. I knew what I was getting into was criminal, and that I'd be finished as a lawyer if I were caught. I didn't care. Irene and I would find a different life, a better life. We could go to America, I would wait tables at night and study during the day, and soon I'd be on top of things again, as a lawyer or doctor, or engineer. If the Americans did not want a convicted lawyer – why not to Mexico? I had found it easy to learn English and French at school; I could learn Spanish easily too.

But before I fell asleep I was shaking; my teeth chattered. I shivered, even after I'd covered my bed with all the blankets I had. Finally, I fell asleep. In the morning I woke up drenched, in a bed soaked with sweat.

And then I felt fine again. I felt light, and at the same time I felt a wild, irresistible power. It was a wonderful, unique feeling. I do not remember having felt that way before or since.

It was Sunday. I ate breakfast on the balcony, the sun was shining, the birds in the trees were singing, and from the church, the bells rang out. I thought about marriage, whether Irene had got married in church, and would want to get married in church, and whether church meant something to her. I dreamed of our shared life in Frankfurt, first on this balcony, then on the balcony of a larger apartment next to the Palm Garden, then in a garden under the old trees on the other side of the river. Then I dreamed of us leaning on the railing of a ship taking us across the Atlantic. I bid farewell to everything: to the firm, to this city, to its people. It was a painless goodbye. For my old life I felt only a friendly indifference.

I left early but I didn't arrive too early. There was a village fête; the square and main road were blocked off and the side streets were clogged with traffic. I parked at the cemetery and found a path through the vineyards which I thought was a shortcut but turned out not to be. In the woods I came across the road that led to Gundlach's neighbourhood. When the first car passed me it occurred to me that Schwind would also take this road, and I could not let myself be seen by him; from then on I followed the road under trees, and through the brush.

I had dressed inconspicuously, in jeans, a beige shirt, a brown leather jacket and sunglasses. But when I emerged from the woods into the neighbourhood, with empty Sunday streets and the occasional family sitting on their terrace under an umbrella, I felt as if all eyes were trained on me; the eyes of the families and other eyes, concealed behind windows. I was the only person on the streets.

I avoided the direct route through the neighbourhood where Schwind could have seen me, but I got lost in the winding side streets, and arrived at the Gundlach house a few minutes after five. The parking space in front of the garage was empty. I hid across the street, between garbage bins and a lilac bush, and waited. I had a view of the driveway, the house, the garage with one door open, one closed, the Mercedes parked in the garage, and on the driveway, a cat lounging in the sun. A couple of small pines grew on the lawn that sloped down from the street to the house, and I planned the zigzag I would run over the lawn, from tree to tree to the car. If someone came by, if someone looked out of the house on the other side of the street – I would have to hide behind the car so quickly they could not be sure they had actually seen me.

I heard Schwind's VW bus from a way off; the exhaust was broken. The van was going fast, coughing, sputtering, it zoomed in from the street and sped up the driveway, scaring off the cat, and abruptly came to a halt in front of the door. No one got out, and after a while the van backed up, made a wide turn around the parking area, backed up again, then finally parked in front of the door, facing the street. The doors opened and they both got out. She was silent, and he ranted. I heard "What does that mean?" and "You and your ideas." Then the front door opened and Gundlach greeted his guests and invited them in.

Now, I said to myself. Anyone who had been drawn to the window by Schwind's noisy VW would be going back to their business by now. I ran across the street, hid behind the first pine, ran again, stumbled, fell, crawled behind the next pine, stood up and ran, limped, hobbled past the last tree to the bus. I opened the door and crouched on the seat so I could not be seen from outside, but could also not see outside. I put the keys in the ignition. I waited.

My foot hurt from the fall, and my back from crouching. But I still felt the lightness and power of the morning, didn't doubt for a second that I was doing the right thing.

Then I heard the front door open and Schwind scolding the butler, who wasn't being quick, careful, or helpful enough. Schwind wasn't pleased that he had to walk around the van, that he had to struggle to open the door. But he got it open, and cursed as he lay the painting in the back, then slid the door shut. As the door clanked shut, I turned the key in the ignition.

The engine started immediately, and by the time Schwind caught on, and yelled, and hit the van, I was off; as he started running, I was already driving fast enough that, though he was able to reach the passenger door and fling it open, he couldn't jump in or even look inside. In the rear-view mirror I watched him running behind me, becoming smaller and smaller until he finally stopped.

# 20

I drove to the bend below Gundlach's house. After a while I got out and walked around the van, opened and closed the sliding door, and shut the passenger door, which I hadn't been able to shut after Schwind threw it open. I didn't want to look at the painting. I don't know why.

Then I stood around, waiting. I looked at the wall Irene planned to climb over. It was about six feet high, white-washed, with a crown of red shingles. The neighbour's tall, dense conifer hedge formed a green wall next to the white one. The fence on the inside of the bend, it too was tall and completely overgrown with ivy, as forbidding as a wall. I looked at the blue sky and heard birds in the gardens, and in the distance, a dog. Everything had a Sunday calm. And yet I felt trapped between the walls. I was freezing, as in the previous night, and was again afraid without knowing what of. That Irene wouldn't come?

Then there she was – light, luminous, laughing, tucking her hair behind her ears, jumping towards me. I caught her in an embrace and thought, now it will all be okay. I was happy and thought she was too. She let me hold her until she caught her breath, then gave me a little kiss and said: "We have to go."

She wanted to drive. And because we might get stuck in the traffic of the village fête, and they might follow and catch up with us, it would be better to take the turn-off, into the hills before the village, and circle around into the city from the east. And because they shouldn't find my car in the village, I should get out before the village and drive my car back to the city.

"How would they recognize my car?"

"We don't want to take any risks."

"Risks? If I go to the village fête, drink some wine, leave my car, and take a taxi back?"

"Do it for my sake, please. I'll feel better that way."

"When will we see each other? What about your things? Don't we have to get them before Schwind comes back? And get the painting out of the van, and park it before he goes to the police?"

"Shhhh," she lay her hand over my mouth. "I'll be careful. And I don't need the few things I have at his place."

"When will you come?"

"Later, when I'm finished."

She dropped me off with a kiss before we reached the village, and I found my car and drove home. Circling around the city, hiding the painting in the place she must have prepared but didn't want to disclose, parking the VW bus and taking a taxi — it would easily be two hours before she came to me. But even before two hours had passed, I was anxious; I paced back and forth in my apartment, looking out the window again and again, and made tea, and forgot to take the leaves out of the pot, and forgot it with the next pot, too. How would she deal with the picture? Wasn't it way too heavy? Was someone helping her? Who? Or would she manage to carry it? Why didn't she trust me?

After two hours I found a reason why she hadn't come. I found another one after three hours, and another after four. Throughout the night I came up with explanations, and tried to quiet my fear that something might have happened to her. With this fear I tried to suppress the deeper fear that she wasn't coming because she didn't want to. The fear that something might have happened – that was the fear of lovers, of close friends, of a mother for her child, and it kept me close to her. When I called the hospitals and police stations before the break of dawn, I claimed I was her husband.

But as dawn broke, I realized that Irene would not come.

# 21

Gundlach called on Monday. "You may have heard this from Schwind. For the record, I want to confirm that my wife has disappeared, and so has the painting. My people will find out if Schwind has double-crossed me. Either way, your services are no longer required."

"I was never in your service."

"Think what you like," he said with a little laugh, and hung up. Several weeks later I received a message that he had no evidence that Schwind had double-crossed him. I thought it was decent of him to let me know. Schwind didn't get in touch again.

I found out that, although her internship wasn't finished, Irene had never gone back to the Museum of Arts and Crafts after the morning we spent together. I also discovered that in addition to the rented flat she'd shared with Schwind, she had another apartment, one she owned, that her friends knew nothing about — a hiding place. The neighbours couldn't remember the last time they had seen her, only that it had been a long time.

I was hurt, sad, furious. I yearned for her and, when I picked up my mail, I sometimes wondered if I would find a letter from her, a postcard. But she never wrote.

Once, two years later, I thought I saw her. Close to our office in Westend, a building had been squatted by students and emptied by the police. The demonstration afterwards, in which thousands of people marched, went by our office, and I stood at the window and looked down. I was surprised at how jubilant the demonstrators were though a supposed injustice had driven them into the streets, how happily they raised their fists, how proudly they shouted slogans, and laughed as they linked arms and fell into a trot. They weren't bad faces: fathers with children on their shoulders, mothers holding their children's hands, many young people, schoolkids and university students, a couple of workers in coveralls, a soldier in uniform, a man in a suit and tie. Then I saw her, or thought I saw her, and ran out of the office and down the stairs and onto the street and alongside the protesters, trying to catch her. A couple of times I thought I saw her. But it wasn't her, and then I found a face similar to hers and thought I'd been tricked by that face, and wanted to give up. But I didn't give up, and looked more, until a group of demonstrators broke into an empty house, and the police came, and the situation escalated.

At some point, wounds scar over. But I never liked to look back on what happened with Irene Gundlach. Especially after I understood what a fool I'd made of myself. How could I not have seen that what had started with a lie could not end well; that I did not belong behind the wheel of a stolen car; that women who ran and climbed away from husbands and lovers were not for me; that I had let myself be used? Anyone with an ounce of sense could have seen that.

I found the ridiculousness of my behaviour most painful when it came back to me how I'd waited at the wall to see if Irene would come or not, want me or not, with my sunglasses, my chills, my fear, and how I had embraced her, and had been happy, and thought she was happy too. I shuddered at the memory.

I've often comforted myself with the thought that, had I not made such a mess of this affair, I could never have run my marriage so successfully. As my wife used to say, every cloud has a silver lining.

The past can't be changed. I made my peace with that long ago. But I find it hard to make my peace with the fact that, again and again, the past doesn't make sense. Maybe every cloud has a silver lining. But every cloud is also just a cloud.

# 22

On Saturday I took the ferry across the bay to the green strip of land and the open sea behind. It wasn't that I had tired of the Botanic Garden. I just thought I shouldn't confine myself to this little habitat, day after day. It was never enough for me to spend my holidays lying on a beach. Instead, I always explored the surrounding area, and I always chose places with interesting surroundings to explore.

The ferry went past a small island, fortified long ago for an imaginary war with some imaginary enemy, past rusty, gray, bobbing warships, past waterfront houses where life was cheerful and light, past woods, a swimming beach here and there, and a marina. The sun, the wind, the smell of the sea – it made for a pleasant morning and, during the tour, children ran tirelessly from fore to aft and aft to fore, where the wind blasted their faces again. I was cold, but was too proud to sit with the old people inside the cabin.

When the boat moored, I got off, and walked up a slope to see the ocean. It looked no different from the Atlantic or Pacific. But I was moved by the idea that it stretched from there to Chile in one direction, and to the Antarctic in the other. When I felt that breadth and depth, the blue of the sea looked darker, the waves washing softly ashore seemed menacing.

I walked along the beach until I tired of the beachside road with its traffic. I went back to where I'd started, and rented a deckchair and a beach umbrella. Once again, I had a bottle of red wine in my backpack, a couple of apples, and my Australian history book.

The history of Australia is short, so the book quickly reached the present day. I learned about the country's climate and natural resources, agriculture, industry and foreign trade, transportation, culture, sport, schools and universities, cuisine, constitution and administration, population density and demographic trends, geographic and social mobility, careers and recreational activities, men and women, divorce rates.

Whenever I'm in a foreign country, I ask myself if I'd be happier there. When I walk down a street and see people standing on a corner, talking and laughing, I imagine that if I lived there, I might stand happily on that corner, talking and laughing. When I walk past an outdoor café and a man walks up to a woman seated at a table, and they greet each other warmly, I think, here I would meet a woman once more who would be happy to see me, as I would be happy to see her. And when the evening lights in the windows go on! Every window promises freedom and safety, freedom from the old life, and safety in a new one. Now, even the simple act of reading awoke a yearning for a different life, in a different world.

Not that I had ever felt shackled to my life. My wife and I made a good team, yet each of us had our freedom. Had she wanted to, she could have worked. We could have afforded a nanny. But she did not want to and, without her, the children would not have turned out as they did; perhaps I would not have either. When she decided to go into local politics, she would not have got as far as she did were it not for my influence. No, I was not shackled. I could never have abandoned everything overnight – house, family, firm – and started out elsewhere. And the colleagues and friends who abandoned marriages and careers, and found a new, younger wife, or a different, more modern job, a thirty-two-year-old event manager replacing a fifty-year-old housewife, a position as a therapist or mediator instead of as a lawyer – after a few years they were back where they'd started: quarreling at home and fed up at work. No, I was not shackled to my life, rather I had chosen it with care, and held on to it with care. It is not as if I couldn't have found a new, younger wife. I do not turn heads, but I keep in shape, and can afford things, I have something to offer a young woman. But I didn't want that.

Odd, how what happened in my life seems both inevitable and to have happened by chance. My choice of career, of wife, of having one child then another and another, my choice of a big law firm – one thing led to the next. I chose my career out of spite; I married because there was no good reason not to. The first decision led to the big law firm; the second, to three children.

# 23

The head of the detective agency called me on Monday. He asked if I was still in Sydney and if I wanted to drop by. It was better, he said, to talk in person.

I spent Sunday in my hotel room. I don't know why I couldn't sleep on Saturday night, why I watched pay-per-view TV – action films, a romance, a family comedy, porn – why I drank whisky, although I usually stick to beer and wine. It was as if I wanted to get drunk. At any rate, I was drunk when I woke on Sunday morning. I stayed in bed and dozed the day away. I had wanted to call my children, but it was too early, and then it was too late.

I do not remember ever having been drunk, much less having intentionally gotten drunk. Of course I had been around drunk people; my partner Karchinger, raised by his cheerful mother from the Rhineland, could have one too many at firm retreats, and hit on the female interns. I had always looked down on him a little for that. I had also looked down on my wife a little when she was drunk, even though her character and circumstances meant she could not have been an alcoholic. I emphasized this after her accident, not only to the police, but also to the children, who even reproached me – as if the shock of her death weren't bad enough. But sometimes I had smelled alcohol on her breath, and her stride and speech were shaky. When she came home at night that way, or I found her at home like that, I slept in my study. Her loud snoring then was unbearable.

I was ashamed of myself when I got up in the evening. I went to the gym, ran on the treadmill, and lifted weights. I was alone, and found the switch to turn off the music, then the one to raise the blinds. I had never seen the harbour and the bay this way. The sky was dark, full of clouds piling up into peaks and ridges. In the distance there were flashes of lightning, sometimes in front of the clouds, like bright scribbling, sometimes behind, lighting their rims white, or blue, or green. Whitecaps danced on the black water. No boat, no ship was out.

I showered, dressed, took the lift to the lobby and walked out of the hotel. Like the bay, the streets were empty. An ambulance drove past, lights flashing and sirens wailing, as if the coming storm had already claimed its first victim. Otherwise it was still. There was no wind. The waves were not choppy, but billowing in from the sea.

I found the calm before the storm depressing, and its arrival a liberation. It swept through the streets and over the square in front of the hotel, driving papers, cups, bags and cans before it – whirling dervishes chasing and over-taking each other. The air chilled and then ice burst from the sky, hailstones that pounded the roof of the entrance, as if wanting to shatter it. I stepped back into the lobby and watched the hail cover the square, a vibrating layer of white.

The staff and guests of the hotel talked about the great hail-storm of 1999, the millions of pieces of hail, their diameter, their damage, their victims. The hailstorm I had seen was small by comparison.

When the hail turned to rain, I went out. The rain fell heavily, and after a few minutes I was wet and clammy. But shuffling through the hail, which the rain was melting, stomping and splashing through the water, making the raindrops fly – it was such a joy that I didn't mind my cold, wet feet or the pain in my side when I slipped and fell. I stood up and went to the harbour, where the rain, sea, land and sky flowed together. It was overwhelming. A flood.

Then the cold and wet became uncomfortable, and I went back to the hotel. I ended Sunday sensibly, slept well, and started Monday sensibly. When the head of the detective agency called, I hailed a cab and drove to him.

# 24

A secretary led me in. He came out from behind the desk, greeted me, offered me the chair opposite, and retreated behind the desk. He was as I had imagined him: an elderly bald man with a paunch. Like all men my age with a paunch and bald head, he made me proud that I had no belly and still had my hair.

"We found her." He settled into the chair and waited for a sign of appreciation.

I had seen this in colleagues. They do what they're supposed to do, the tasks they have been assigned and for which they are being paid. But they cannot simply deliver results, they want to be fussed over, and patted on the head. Sometimes they try to make a game of it and have the results teased out of them. In my firm I drove such bad habits out of my colleagues. I would not be able to drive them out of the head of the detective agency. I nodded in appreciation and asked excitedly: "Where is she?"

"It wasn't easy. She's lived here for twenty years. But . . ." He paused, shook his head, and only continued when I repeated: "But?"

"But she's an illegal. She entered the country as a tourist, and did not sort out anything – residency permit, work

67

permit, citizenship, health insurance, nothing. We haven't tracked down where she's been for the past twenty years or what she's been doing. Today she lives on the coast, north of here – three, four hours away. She must have money in Germany, she pays with a German credit card. That is why she's slipped through the net. If she had worked here and opened a bank account and ordered a credit card, she would have needed to present papers she didn't have."

"What name does she go by?"

"Irene Adler. Her maiden name and a name that sounds good in both languages, English and German. I hear her English is perfect."

"What do you know about her connection to the art gallery?"

"She offered the curator her painting, and he accepted. He did some research and didn't see any problems. The painting is mentioned in an early catalogue of Karl Schwind's work, and isn't on the international registry of stolen art. Since then other museums have shown an interest, and the *New York Times* wrote a long article about the rediscovered masterpiece."

It sounded as though his agency had found someone at the art gallery who had abused the curator's trust and had looked into his files; and they had then looked into the immigration agency files; and finally asked around where Irene Gundlach lived. I had hoped for more. I had hoped I would learn where she had lived, how she was living now, who she was now. At the same time I knew that hope was foolish. I had not asked for that, just whether the picture belonged to her, and if she lived in Australia.

I took down the address, Red Cove in Rock Harbour,

thanked him, and paid. On the way to the hotel I bought a pair of cotton trousers, a pair of linen trousers, shorts, and shirts. The hotel found me a rental car, and after I had packed and thanked them, I paid and set off.

# 25

I could still have made it to Rock Harbour on Monday. After I had survived a couple of close scrapes as I made turns, or passed, I adjusted to driving on the left. I drove elatedly, first on a six-lane motorway, and then on a two-lane road that sometimes hugged the coast, sometimes diverged from it. And suddenly my courage vanished.

I pulled onto the shoulder, stopped, and got out. What did I want from Irene Gundlach, or Irene Adler? To tell her that I still resented her? To finally tell her in person what I had said in my thoughts? That it is not right to use people and drop them? That I had been too naïve and awkward, but that I had loved her nonetheless, and that it is not right to play with someone else's love? That she could at least have written me a letter, an explanation to ease the sting?

I would only make a fool of myself again. It all happened forty years ago; she would think I was an idiot who was stuck in the past. I myself found it idiotic, how present the past was to me. It was as if we had sat on the bench by the Main River only yesterday, as if only yesterday I had waited for her in the VW bus, only yesterday that she dropped me off outside the village. As if I would still be the person I was back then, when we sat on a bench together now.

Is that how it is with things that don't quite come to an end? But things do not come to an end, one has to bring them to an end. I should have brought that episode to an end back then; I should have given it a meaning. I had wanted to convince myself that without Irene things would have not gone so well with my wife, but it wasn't true. I had filed away my schooldays and university years, my deceased mother, my father who visited me at my grandparents' a couple of times before moving to Hong Kong and dying there, as things that were as they were, and couldn't have been different. Why did something inside me insist things could have turned out differently with Irene?

I had stopped on a rise. To the west, the mountains were covered in brush and scrub, straight trees and bowed trees. The upright trees had pale, barkless trunks, as if naked or sick. The sea lay to the east, beyond two mountain ridges. I crossed the road and sat down on the embankment. The sea was dappled, gray and blue, smooth and rough. In the distance, two ships were sailing but appeared to be staying in the same spot.

Sailing and staying in the same spot – that was how I felt. Then I said to myself that it only appeared as if the ships were staying in the same spot. Perhaps I too was moving even though it didn't seem that way to me. I thought of the spots on my suit and had to laugh. These stains, which would have alarmed me before, hadn't frightened me since the afternoon at the Botanic Garden. Yes, I had moved from the spot. Making a fool of myself in front of Irene Gundlach, or Irene Adler, would matter no more than having a stain on my suit.

The sun was shining. The air smelled of pine and eucalyptus.

I thought I could also smell the distant sea, a weak, damp, salty scent. I heard the cicadas chirr and sometimes, in the valley, the roar of a saw. I decided not to worry. I would drive to Rock Harbour the next day, but today, find a hotel by the sea and watch the spectacle of the sunset from the terrace. In Australia day turns to night in only a few minutes, bright blue becoming dark blue, then black.

# 26

Rock Harbour had four streets, a small harbour with a few yachts and boats, a shop with a café and a postal counter, a real-estate agency, and an iron soldier on a stone pedestal, commemorating those who fell in the World Wars, the Korean War, the Vietnam War. The streets were empty, but not because of the early hour, as I initially thought, but rather because the summer houses were still without tenants. I found neither a street nor a house that went by the name "Red Cove". I went into the shop and asked.

"You want to see Eye-reen?" A man with white skin, white hair and pink eyes who sat by the counter lay down his book and stood up. Eye-reen? His way of saying her name was not mine: in German it was three short syllables, three bright vowels, three notes of a waltz — a name meant to be sung, to be danced to. For me, "Eye-reen" sounded stretched out like chewed gum. "She lives an hour from here. Do you have a boat?"

"I have my car."

"You can only get there by boat. You could wait for her here, but she only comes every two weeks and she was here yesterday. You can't call either, there's no reception there."

"Are there ships that go along the coast?"

He laughed. "A ferry service? No, we don't have that. My boy can take you over in the boat. He can also pick you up if you know when you want to be picked up."

"I'll call."

"Nope, can't call."

"Can your boy take me, right away? And pick me up tonight?" This time, the man had let me finish my sentence.

He nodded and invited me to wait for his son, Mark, at one of the tables on the terrace. I took a seat and waited, listening to him on the telephone. Then he brought over two beers, sat down next to me and introduced himself. He had lived in Sydney, had had enough of the city, and had moved here seven years ago. He loved the sea, the tranquility, how the sleepy small town awoke in summer, the hustle and bustle of the summer months, the off-peak season, when artists and writers rented more cheaply for a couple of weeks, the return of calm. Everyone came to him: young families, grandparents, teenagers, artists.

"Living where she does wouldn't be my cup of tea. It's beautiful, but a lonely beauty . . . not a single soul, far and wide. What brings you to her?"

"We haven't seen each other in a long time."

"I know." He laughed. "Otherwise you'd have already met me. When did you last see her?"

"Many years ago."

He didn't pry further. Mark arrived, took me to an old-fashioned launch, started up the motor, and cast off. He stood in the cabin and steered; I sat on the bench in front of the cabin, facing the sun and wind. The mountains and the coves all looked the same, and the boat rose and fell with a gentle rhythm, slapping the water, as the motor chugged with the same, calm rhythm. I fell asleep.

# Part Two

# 1

I woke up to Mark cutting the engine. The boat drifted into a cove, towards a jetty. Just before we reached it, Mark fired up the engine again, guiding the boat towards the end of the jetty, then moored.

"This evening at six?"

"Yes." I jumped from the boat. Mark cast off and drove away. I watched him until he rounded the cape and disappeared from view. Then I turned around.

The house on the beach was a one-storey stone house. The roof of the veranda rested on stone columns and was tiled in slate. It looked as if it had stood there a long time and intended to stay there; as if, with this house, civilization had carved a bridgehead in the wilderness that it was prepared to defend.

As I headed down the jetty towards the house, I saw another house, wooden, two-storey, built on the hillside with a view to the sea, that was so tucked into the trees that you couldn't see it from afar. As solidly as the stone house sat on the beach, the other one hung on the mountain provisionally. The timbers supporting the house tilted at such unlikely angles that they startled the eye. The roof and balcony were bowed, some of the window frames so warped that it must have been impossible to close the windows. They were all open, along with all the doors. A curtain fluttered out of one of the windows.

The door of the beach house was closed. I knocked, waited and finally went inside, entering a large room with an old iron stove and an old iron range, a hutch, a table, a couple of chairs and, through a door into a second smaller room, a bed, a nightstand and a wardrobe. The rooms didn't look lived in – did Irene live up above in summer, and only come down here when it was cold? From the large room, another door led out behind the house to a pump and an outhouse.

I looked up at the other house. Nothing had changed, all the doors and windows were still open and the curtain was still fluttering in the wind. I sensed that I would not find Irene up there. I could go from room to room, shouting her name, to see her place, and get a sense of her life, but I didn't want to do that. She had built a terrace onto the slope, where a vegetable patch was planted with lettuce, beans, tomato plants and raspberry bushes. It needed watering.

Suddenly, I had the impression that everything was lifeless. Abandoned. As if whoever had lived here had departed in haste, never to return, inviting the wind to sweep through the house, the rain to seep into the rooms, the floors to rot, the pillars to crumble. The fluttering curtain reminded me of photos of ruins, where a bomb has ripped off the side of a building, leaving rooms and their furniture, pictures, and curtains exposed.

The sun went behind a cloud, and a cooler wind blew in from the sea. The water in the cove lay gray and cold. I put on the sweater I had around my shoulders, but I was still chilled. I found a musty wool blanket on the bed, wrapped it around me, sat down on the bench on the veranda, leant my head against the wall, and waited.

# 2

I didn't hear Irene's boat come in. I had fallen asleep again.
I heard her only when she sat down next to me and said:
"My brave knight!"

I kept my eyes shut. Her voice sounded as it had then, dark
and smoky and, as then, I couldn't sense what it conveyed.
Was she making fun of me? I felt indignant, but indignation
was no way to begin. "Shining armour? This knight is tired,
he is hungry and thirsty. Do you have anything to eat and
drink?" I opened my eyes and looked at her.

She laughed and stood up. I recognized her laughter too,
by its sound and by her face, the way her eyes squinted, the
dimples in her cheeks, her lopsided mouth. As she became
serious, I took in that her eyes were blue-gray – back then, I
had only registered that they were light. I saw all the wrinkles on her forehead and cheeks, her heavy eyelids, the tired
skin and thinning hair. Irene had grown old, and I can't say
if I'd have recognized her had we crossed paths on the street.
But like her voice and her laugh, the way she tucked her hair
behind her ears, and the tilt of her head, were familiar. She
had grown fuller around the waist, and I asked myself if the
teenagers had seen something I hadn't, in her hips and legs.
She was wearing jeans, a T-shirt, and a plaid woollen shirt

like a jacket. She had put down a bucket of fish she'd caught; I picked it up and followed her to the upper house.

As we went up, first up a path, then a wooden stairway – like the stairs from the beach up the dunes – Irene started breathing heavily. She leant on my arm and more than once had to take a break.

"Maybe I'll move back down into the lower house," she said, once we were inside. "It's cold in winter, but it's nice and cool in summer."

"It has a stove."

She looked at me. I didn't know whether she was still sizing me up or was already disappointed, but I could tell what she was thinking: that lawyer can't listen, he has to tell me I have a stove, as if I didn't know that.

"That was a stupid thing to say."

She smiled. "I don't usually need to heat up here in the winter. Down there, the stone walls hold in the cold. It was a postal station, built more than a hundred years ago for the farms in the outback. The farms are long gone; the soil is poor and, one by one, the farmers gave up. The outback is now a nature reserve. I think the last mail boat came at Christmas, 1951." The sweeping gesture of her arm encompassed the room we were standing in, the crooked door, the crooked windows, the crooked beams that carried the weight of the top floor, and the crooked stairs that led to it. "You don't need to tell me that it will fall apart soon, I know. But that day hasn't come just yet."

The room – kitchen, dining room and living room all in one – took up the entire ground floor. The range with six hobs, the table to seat twelve, the three sofas made it much too big for Irene. I refrained from enquiring further, and let her show me how to scale fish. I peeled potatoes, washed the lettuce and made a salad dressing; I can't cook, but I can make a good dressing. Irene asked what I had been doing in Sydney, what I did in Frankfurt, asked after my wife and children and whether I was content with my life. I didn't want to give away any more about myself than she did, but she turned any of the few questions I managed to ask into a question of her own, giving nothing away. And yet, when we were finally sitting on the balcony, eating, we had created a bit of intimacy − while cooking, talking, the moments when we'd touched, when I held her as she used a ladder to get a bottle of oil from a high cupboard, when I helped her with a blocked drain and a sticky drawer.

I saw the boat before I heard it. I had not looked at the time once. As the putter of the engine came into earshot, Irene said: "You didn't come here for no reason. When do you want to talk?"

"I'll come again tomorrow."

"You can stay here. There are six empty rooms upstairs. I'll find pyjamas and overalls for you, so you don't get your clothes dirty when you help me tomorrow."

So I went down to the jetty and talked to Mark. He asked whether I didn't want to give him my car keys. Then he could bring my luggage with him tomorrow. In case I stayed longer.

# 3

By the time I had got back to the balcony, she had cleared the table and opened a bottle of red.

"Did Schwind want to keep all his paintings, or just the one of you?" I wanted to tread lightly.

"He wanted to keep the pictures he felt defined him as an artist. That spoke to issues in contemporary painting: what representation and abstraction can offer, their relationship to photography, how beauty and truth interact."

"And your painting?"

"It was an answer to Marcel Duchamp. Do you know *Nude Descending a Staircase?* A cubist figure, breaking up in the moments of descent, a vortex of legs, ass, arms and heads? Duchamp's work was talked about as the end of painting, and Schwind wanted to show that a naked woman descending a staircase could still be painted."

I did not understand. "Why should what Duchamp painted be the 'end of painting'?"

"You came here so you could finally understand modern art?" She smiled amicably, but behind the friendliness was something I couldn't tease out. Was it contempt, rejection, exhaustion? The thought entered my mind that people say "dead tired" when they are very tired but full of life, but when they use "tired of life", they're near the end.

"I want to understand what happened. I made it easy for you. But you used me, and you let me know that clearly. You could have called or written a letter or a postcard. If you felt you had to use me and hurt me, why didn't you—"

"Package it in friendliness?" She spoke now with open contempt. "For Gundlach I was the young, blonde, beautiful trophy, only the packaging counted. For Schwind, I was a muse, the packaging was enough for that too. Then you came along. A woman's third stupid role, after the trophy and the muse, is the damsel in distress who must be rescued by the prince. To stop her falling into the hands of the villain, the prince takes her into his own hands. After all, she belongs in the hands of some man." She shook her head. "No, I wasn't interested in friendly packaging."

"I never forced a role on you. When I approached you, you could have kindly refused me and gone on your way."

"Kindly refused . . ."

"An unfriendly refusal then. In any case, you didn't have to use me."

She nodded, tired now. "Roles make you predictable, interchangeable, useable. The prince who saves the princess – you used me just as much as Gundlach and Schwind."

My firm employs more women than the statistical average. We operate our own kindergarten with the tax advisors on the floor below us and the accountants on the floor above. I supported my wife's career and, after my daughter studied art history, I also paid for a law degree. I don't need to be lectured on feminism.

"Are you trying to tell me that the only choices you had were trophy, muse or princess? Between what Gundlach,

Schwind and I wanted from you? With your money and your career, you had every opportunity to find your own identity. Don't shove responsibility—"

"Responsibility? You don't want to understand, you want to judge." She looked at me in disbelief. "Is that what matters to you? That you can judge me? That you can have a clear conscience? Your life must surely add up to more than just 'not guilty'!"

I didn't understand what she wanted from me.

"Is this what happens to someone who spends their life with law? It doesn't matter who you are any more, only that you're in the right? And that the other is in the wrong?"

Night had fallen, again it had only taken minutes. But the night wasn't black; the moon cast a silver light on the leaves and the sea. It shone on Irene's face, highlighting its tiredness, its wrinkles and sagging so mercilessly that I felt pity for her – and myself. We were old, it was all such a long time ago. Why worry her, why worry myself with this old affair?

But I couldn't leave that old affair behind so easily. Just as I was admitting it to myself, she said: "I'm sorry that I hurt you. I felt so caged that all I wanted was to break free. I didn't care about anything else. When I think back . . . you were still such a child."

# 4

If I had still been a child then, what was I now? Lying in bed, Irene's remark kept me awake. Of course, I know far more about human nature and how to handle people now than I did then; what one owes them, what one should not put up with, how to act during negotiations and how to act in court. But I knew it all then too, the rudiments at least, and I hadn't felt like a child.

The small room that Irene had given me faced the sea. If I listened closely, I could hear in the silence the waves washing ashore, the rush as they came in, the rustle through the pebbles as they retreated. The room was lit with moonlight; I could clearly see the cupboard, the chair, the mirror.

If I listened closely, I thought I could hear Irene's breathing. But that couldn't be; there was another room between hers and mine. But if I wasn't hearing her breathing, I was hearing the house breathe, and that was even more impossible. A steady, heavy flow in and out. Then I heard an animal screech, a cry that peeled out as if the creature had awoken from a nightmare, or been petrified by something awful.

Or it had been startled by the wind that suddenly kicked up. Out of nothing it blew around the house, shaking it until the beams creaked. I got up and went to the window, expecting the first drops. But the sky was clear and the moon shone. The wind brought no rain with it; it only bent the trees and made the house groan.

The wind felt weird. It came without clouds, and without rain; it had no right to show off, but it did. It did not blow on me, but around me and through me and let me know how frail I was, as it let the house feel how fragile it was. Then things became even weirder. On the balcony someone was squatting, and turned their face towards me. A boy with dark skin and short hair, a broad nose and wide mouth, his feet on the ground, knees bent, his bottom hovering above the ground. I would tip over backwards, I thought, if I were to squat like that. His eyes must be deep-set, I thought, since I couldn't see the whites. But I saw that he had fixed me in an unmoving, inscrutable gaze.

Should I wake Irene? If the boy planned to rob us, alone or with others, or to set the house on fire – it didn't fit with his calm posture or the bright moon or the roar of the wind. The weird feeling had come over me not because I was afraid. It was because I didn't understand what everything here meant – the boy, the wind, what Irene had said, what kept me here.

# 5

When I awoke, the sky was still pale. I heard a loud rustling, went to the window and saw a flock of blackbirds circling above the trees, close and loud, then distant and soft, and when the flock was distant and soft I heard the other birds, which sang the same three notes over and over again, or repeated the same short caw, or chirped the same trembling staccato. I imagined their bills desperately held open, until the flock surged back and drowned them out.

A pair of overalls had appeared on the chair, in the same way the pyjamas had appeared on the bed the previous day. I heard Irene descend the stairs slowly, then start working in the kitchen. I got dressed.

Over coffee, Irene explained that her Jeep had a flat tyre and the crank on the jack was broken. I needed to lift the Jeep so she could push a stone underneath and change the tyre.

"They told me no roads lead here."

"When they made the area a nature reserve the roads were abandoned. Where they joined the road network, they were blocked off. But the old tracks are enough for a Jeep, and you can drive around the barriers. We insiders know how to get out, the people out there, luckily, don't know how to get in."

"We?"

"There are still two farmsteads. That's where I need to go later."

The Jeep was too heavy for me. The piece of wood I tried to use as a lever broke. Finally, I found an iron pipe, managed to lever up the Jeep, and Irene slid a stone underneath. The rest was easy, even if I couldn't remember the last time I had changed a tyre.

On the way, I asked Irene about the boy who had squatted on the balcony in the night. Kari used to live with her and came from time to time to make sure everything was okay. She could tell that I wanted to know more.

"I used to take in children – abandoned kids, strays, drug addicts, alcoholics. Not officially, not through social services or child services, I'm not here officially myself, but word got around among the children. Some came for a few days or weeks, to rest a while, some stayed for a year or two. A couple of them managed to get back into school or into work. Others returned in a worse state than when they'd left. If they were still under eighteen, I took them back in. No one over eighteen, that was the iron rule."

"How many children did you have?"

"The house has seven rooms, and there was a child in each, occasionally two. I lived downstairs."

"What did you all live on?"

"We had chickens and goats, grew all sorts of produce, the farms helped us, and sometimes the children brought stuff they had stolen. They learned that you have to share and that you can't steal for yourself, only for the group."

It was a bumpy conversation. Irene drove quickly and confidently, steering the Jeep steadily over every bump in the road, through washed-out riverbeds and dried-out ponds, sometimes straight through the underbrush; the trail kept disappearing and appearing again. I was thrown up, and from side to side; I wedged my foot against the chassis and held fast to the seat, wishing the Jeep had a roof or at least a door that closed. But it was open, an old Jeep straight from a war film.

"Where did you get the Jeep?"

She laughed. "Stolen. In the beginning we had to lug everything around. One day Arunta and Arthur turned up with the Jeep. A collector had had it in his garage. They had been with me a year and had turned eighteen, and knew they couldn't stay. But they wanted to make life easier for the rest of us." She laughed again. "I don't think much of collecting. Do you?"

Then we reached a valley with a stream that was almost dried up, and meadows and trees and cows, which gathered in the shade of a willow, like in a seventeenth-century Dutch painting. At the end of the valley lay the first farm. A large wooden house with two barns, some young men and women, lots of children, pigs and hens – I was greeted briefly, then ignored. Irene went into the house, and after a while I followed her. I found her in the kitchen; she was taking a dressing off a girl's shoulder. She examined the wound, applied ointment from a small tin, and put on a new dressing. "She wanted to smash through the wall with her shoulder," she said when she saw me, "she won't do it again. Right? You won't do that again?" The girl shook her head.

92

The other farm felt abandoned. The old lady who opened the door gave me a hostile, suspicious look, took Irene by the hand, pulled her inside the house and shut the door. I sat in the Jeep, taking in the decrepit house, the dilapidated barn and the rusty equipment, fighting the despondency that enveloped the farm, and wanted to envelop me too.

# 6

"He won't last much longer," said Irene as she sat back down next to me.

"And then?"

She drove off. "Then she won't last much longer either, and the young people from the other farm will finally take over. They would have done it long ago and looked after the old folks, but they don't want it. They've turned nasty." She shrugged her shoulders. "We here are no better than you out there. At first I thought so. But it's not true."

"Did you become a doctor?"

"Nurse. That's enough for most things. Without equipment, I'd be no use as a doctor."

I imagined the scenarios, the burst appendix, the heart attack, cancer. I wondered how they taught the children; where they got their pens and paper and books. What else would the people here need from the outside world? How did the people at the first farm know each other? Were the young families who lived in the same house a commune, a sect? What had Irene looked for here, and what had she found?

"I used other people, even worse than I did you."

"Did you take their money? Their reputation? Their life?"

I said it flippantly, each outcome seemed as absurd as the next.

She laughed.

I did not like her laugh. She laughed the way you'd laugh at a bad joke, or a nasty trick, or some bad luck that you would rather cry about.

She said nothing. I had nothing to say either. Although the drive through the bush didn't invite conversation, the silence between us was loud. When we arrived and she had parked, she stayed seated.

"Will you help me up to my room? I can't make it alone."

She had parked the Jeep above the house, and on the way down, she leant on my right arm. But then I had to put both arms around her to hold and guide her. The stairs in the house were steep and narrow; Irene said since she often took the stairs on all fours, like a dog, she could let herself be carried by me like a dog as well. I picked her up, carried her upstairs and laid her on her bed.

"I'm sorry," she said, "I overdid it. When I do everything nice and slowly, it's okay. But I'm no good at doing that. I overdo it, then my legs go weak and don't want to carry me, and sometimes my head doesn't want to go on either."

I fetched the chair and sat down next to the bed. "What do you have?"

"My brave knight," she smiled, "nothing you can save me from. Just let me sleep a little."

She closed her eyes. Her breathing became regular, sometimes her eyelids fluttered, sometimes her hands wandered over her belly, saliva pooled in the corner of her mouth. She smelled sick, not sick the way my children did when they had their childhood colds, or flus, or stomach aches. Irene smelled strong, strange, repulsive.

What was I still doing here? I knew what I had needed to know. She was even sorry that she had used me – what more did I want?

I got up quietly, left the house and went down to the beach. My luggage was on the jetty, with a note stuck in the zip of my travel bag. Mark had come in the morning, because he would be held up in the afternoon and evening; he was sorry he'd missed me and been unable to bring me back, but at least he'd brought my bag.

# 7

I sat down on the bench on the veranda of the house by the beach. While I had sat by Irene's bed, the sky had clouded over. Rain clouds? I felt a chill and fetched the musty blanket. Sitting here again, cold again, smelling the blanket again – it seemed that time was standing still and I was too.

No, Irene would not be living here, like this, if she had taken someone's money. If she had ruined someone's reputation, the newspapers hadn't caught on, so it couldn't have been anything too bad. And if she had taken a life, I would have read about that in the papers too. Or had she committed the perfect murder? Irene?

I had never felt the desire to kill anyone, be they a competitor or an adversary, a child molester or child killer, Pinochet or Kim Jong-il. Not that I set such a high value on life. The value of life remains a mystery to me. How can one define the value of something lost, if the person who has lost it doesn't miss it? But of course I abhor violence. Bludgeoning or stabbing someone to death – hideous, and that someone sets off a bomb from afar that tears the victim apart is no less hideous. Perhaps it is even more hideous: an act of violence that divests itself of all the feelings and inhibitions that arise from closeness.

I have never dealt with murderers. My firm doesn't take criminal defence cases. But I simply couldn't imagine Irene as a murderer. She knew how to keep her cool; she knew how to get her way. I could think of nothing that would have driven her to murder. Even if her second husband had seen her as no more than a trophy, like her first, even if her next lover had also wanted to take advantage of her, if the manager whose advances she had rejected demoted her or her neighbour had harassed her in the hall – Irene would have known how to deal with all of it. If someone had tried to rob or attack her, it would have been self-defence, nothing she could have been reproached for or that she would have had to reproach herself for. So what was she talking about?

I was making the same mistake I had back then. At the time I had assumed I knew who she was, yet I knew nothing. Our intimacy had existed only in my imagination. Once again, I was imagining that I could feel and think my way into her head, that we were close. Why? Only because she had walked naked into my life? In a painting?

I stood up, folded the blanket, went up to the house on the hillside and into the kitchen. In the pantry cupboard I found spaghetti, tins of tomatoes and a glass of olives, and anchovies and capers in the spice rack. Cooking doesn't come easy to me, but I wasn't in a hurry. By the time I heard Irene get up and walk to the stairs, the table was set and the meal was ready. I helped her down the steps, led her to the table and served her food. She looked at me; I was proud and she saw my pride and smiled.

"You're still here."

"The boat came while we were out, left my luggage and went back. Now you'll have to take me to Rock Harbour."

"When?"

I shrugged my shoulders. "Tomorrow?"

"Whenever you like."

# 8

That annoyed me. Could she not have said: You don't have to go, you can stay if you want? "Did things have to go the way they did? Could they have gone differently?"

She looked at me, astonished. "My brave—"

"Drop the 'brave knight' bit. I loved you. You told me then that I had never been in love – do you remember? – and you were right, I never had, that was my first time. I was a bit clumsy, I know, but I'm not complaining, that would be ridiculous. All I want to know is whether I could have done something better, and if so, could things have worked out between us."

"You mean, could I have been part of your law firm life in Frankfurt, with golf clubs, tennis, a subscription to the opera?"

"We could have gone abroad, to America or Brazil or Argentina. I would have settled in quickly and learned the language and the legal system and—"

"And soon you'd have had a prosperous legal firm and joined the high society of wherever we ended up."

"What's wrong with that?"

"Have you ever represented normal people – workers, renters, people whose health was ruined, battered women?

Have you ever brought a case against the state? The police, the church? Have you defended political activists? Have you ever risked anything? I was looking for someone like that. Someone who would take a risk, someone I could take a risk with. Even life itself. What did you say yesterday? Mergers and acquisitions? Who cares who merges with whom, and who acquires whom? Not even you can be interested in that. You enjoy the fact that you can do it, that other people aren't getting one over on you because you're getting one over on them. You like the money, the fancy hotels, the first-class flights. Did you ever stop to think about the real world, about justice in the real world?"

"There can be justice and injustice in mergers and acquisitions."

"Have you never dreamed of more? Of justice for the exploited and the oppressed? Tell me you haven't always been this way."

I poked around in my spaghetti and focused on eating. She ate too, but kept her eyes on me and waited for an answer. What was I supposed to say? I was proud of my pragmatism; the most extravagant fantasy I'd had in my entire life had been to move with her to Buenos Aires, serve drinks by night and study by day – and soon be back on top. If that hadn't worked out, if I'd been stuck in Buenos Aires with Irene, living in a hole, scraping by with third-rate cases, engaging with abstruse political causes – I didn't want to imagine that life.

"Yes, I always was. I dreamed of moving to Buenos Aires with you and studying by day and serving drinks by night, and for a new life with you, I would have become a gaucho, or washed dishes in New York or been a lumberjack in the Rockies. But at the end of the dream was the good life. The exploited and oppressed – they have to figure out their problems themselves."

She looked at the plate. "It tastes good." We ate. I served her another helping and refilled the wine and water glasses. After a while she said: "Don't have any regrets. You couldn't have done anything different back then. You would have had to be a different person."

# 9

When I returned to the table after clearing it and washing the dishes, Irene was asleep, her head on her arm. The last time I carried her to her room she had made herself light, this time she lay heavy in my arms. I set her down on the bed, took off her shoes, jeans, and heavy shirt, then tugged the covers out from under her and tucked her in.

The rain I had expected had not arrived, and I sat on the balcony. From time to time the moon peeked out from between the clouds and made the sea sparkle. Otherwise, it was dark. The cicadas were as loud as a tree full of birds.

Irene had gone too far. I would have had to be someone else? I should have dreamed of justice for the exploited and oppressed and not just dreamed of it, but lived for it?

It takes many masons to build the cathedral of justice; some hew blocks, others carve plinths and cornices, still others, ornaments and statues. They are all equally important to the project: prosecution and defence are as important as judgement; the drafting of rental, employment and inheritance contracts is as important as the implementation of mergers and acquisitions; the lawyer for the rich as important as the lawyer for the poor. The cathedral would still rise without my contribution. It would rise without this cornice, or that ornament, but still they are part of it.

I suddenly imagined Irene's mocking question. How did I know I was building a cathedral and not an apartment building, a shopping mall, a prison?

Something came back to me. I had only just started at Karchinger and Kunze when I took on the defence of a guy I knew at school and university. He had gone back to our school and convinced several of the students to take part in a demonstration. He was leading them from the schoolyard when a teacher stepped in their way, there was a scuffle, the teacher fell and was injured. Did my old schoolmate have no money for an attorney? Did he challenge me by saying that defending him would be too much for me? Was he flattering me, that I would be the perfect choice to defend him? In any case, I took him on. I did it pro bono, informing only the firm manager, not Karchinger and Kunze. But they caught wind of it and they were furious. I was defending someone who had incited a riot – what would our corporate and industry clients think? I had to give up the case, and although I found a replacement, the prosecution won. The fact that I gave up the case right after the teacher was admitted to hospital, and the defendant faced conviction on an even more serious charge, made it look as though I was distancing myself from my old schoolmate. That did nothing to help his defence.

Would I have obtained an acquittal? I was confident; I wanted to win my first and presumably only criminal case, so I had hired a private investigator and learned that the furious janitor had started the scuffle, and that the teacher had previously suffered epileptic fits. I had told all this to my replacement, but he had not been good enough. Perhaps someone else would have been better – and more expensive. I had promised my former schoolmate that I would pay the costs.

He could not have afforded the lawyer I found him, let alone a better one. I owed him nothing. We had been friends in school and during the first few semesters at university, but that was a long time ago. He was an eternal student. I did not want to idle away my life, so soon we had nothing in common. At the time, sentences in political cases were draconian, and he was sent to prison without probation. Maybe it was not so bad for him, maybe it didn't make a difference to him whether he idled away his days inside prison or outside. I didn't visit him in prison, and he never got in touch again. What became of him?

I am in nobody's debt. Nor do I owe anyone a debt of gratitude. When I get something, I find a way to reciprocate. When someone is generous to me, I return the favour double or threefold. I can safely say that I don't profit from my relationships with friends and acquaintances. At work it's different, but there you don't have anyone's generosity to thank for the profit on your balance sheet, only your own hard work.

It was raining. I stood in the doorway and listened to the rain. But then I heard a strange noise upstairs, and went up. The wind had blown the curtain in Irene's room away from the window, and the wet fabric was slapping against the outside wall. I pulled the curtain back in and struggled to close the warped window.

Irene slept fitfully. I lit the candle next to the bed, and I saw the same restless hands and fluttering eyelids, and the sweat on her brow and above her upper lip. Occasionally she murmured something that I did not understand. I wiped the sweat from her face. As I shook out the blanket to cover her better, I saw that her T-shirt and underpants were soaked through with sweat. Find pyjamas and a towel, get her out of those wet things, dry her off and get her into the pyjamas – that's what needed to be done. But I stood there looking at her and thought, What do I have to do with this woman?

I did what needed to be done anyway. I found pyjamas in the wardrobe and towels in the bathroom. When I lifted Irene and took off her T-shirt, she put her arms around my neck without saying a word, without opening her eyes, without waking up. When I slipped on the pyjama top she did the same. She probably just wanted to make it easier for me to lift her, as she had learned as a nurse and had taught her patients. But it touched me as a childlike, tender gesture. I got her out of her undergarments, and, before putting her pyjamas on, dried her off: her shoulders, her chest, her belly, her thighs. She must have weighed more, once; her skin was too big for her body. Once again I smelled the scent of illness.

Occasionally, I catch sight of my naked body in the mirror and pity it. All it has been through, how it has struggled, the pain it has endured. I have no self-pity, I despise that. It's not me I pity, it's my body. Or decay in general. Now, I pitied Irene's body. So frail, vulnerable, needy, so trusting when she lay her arms around my neck. I felt sorry for it. Still, I was annoyed that she hadn't invited me to stay longer.

# 10

Over breakfast Irene talked about her plans for the day. She needed to give the old man an injection. She wanted to bake bread with the young people; Thursday was baking day. She didn't offer to take me to Rock Harbour, and I didn't ask her to. As I accompanied her to the Jeep, she said: "I'll be back at the same time as yesterday, hopefully in better shape. Are you cooking again?"

Again, I sat on the bench on the veranda. Unlike in the last days, the sun was shining, I wasn't cold and I didn't need a blanket. And yet, I again had the feeling that time was standing still and I was too.

I needed to make decisions. I needed to call my firm. I needed to delegate work. A good firm runs like a machine in which every cog starts at the right moment and stops at the right moment. If one cog fails, another replaces it. For a long time I had thought that I was the drive belt, and when the drive belt fails, the machine runs a little longer, then starts to grind, then shudders, then comes to a halt. But there is no drive belt, there are only cogs, and even a big cog is soon replaced, either with another big cog or with a couple of small ones. If I was absent for a while the firm wouldn't grind to a halt. But it just isn't done, to simply be absent. If a senior partner doesn't act like he is irreplaceable, the other partners start feeling dispensable too and lose their motivation.

Really, it would be best if everyone had to work but could choose the moment when they stopped working. For three years afterwards, society would cover the costs of a decent, comfortable life. Then they would have to take their leave from the world. How they did it would be up to them.

I know, that will never come to pass. But it wouldn't just solve the problem of our ageing society. It would give everyone control over their life. If someone wants to stop working at twenty-six and make the last years of their youth the last years of their life and enjoy them to the fullest, they would be allowed to stop working at twenty-six; and those who can't let go of work can keep working as long as they want, only running the risk that one day they'll be too old to enjoy their three years of leisure.

In any case, I ask only for three years at the end of my working life, nothing more. I cannot understand the pensioners who travel to China and spend two days in Shanghai, three in Beijing, one at the Great Wall, and five days on the beach at Qingdao. They don't see any more on holiday than they would on TV. They go home and tell the other pensioners holiday stories they already know. They tell their children things they do not want to know. When they want to enjoy their memories, because they cannot travel any more, they will already have forgotten them. To grow old, to see the world – how stupid. Growing old to see how the world develops or to watch your grandchildren grow up – that's also stupid. Why start reading a book when you know you will not be able to read it to the end, but will have to close it in the middle and put it to one side?

Three years of such stupidities are enough. Three years! I thought, but could not think what stupidities I would fill three years with. Nor did any reason come to mind as to why I should worry about mergers and acquisitions again. These two findings made me feel uneasy. Until I fell asleep, warm and drowsy from the sun.

# 11

The helicopter woke me. It did not come over the mountain, but along the coast, turning into the cove and circling around the beach and the jetty. Then it turned out of the cove just as it had come. It flew low and loud, and the rattling, hissing rotor blade churned up the ocean.

The helicopter was unmarked, and bore no sign of belonging to the police or rescue services, or a TV network. The shining metal, the mirrored glass, the loud, low approach over the churning sea — it felt like an attack. I stood up, frightened and confused. The secret service? What was Irene mixed up in? She was in the country illegally, but for that the secret service doesn't send a helicopter, but maybe it was not secret service, maybe it was organized crime, either way she must have been involved in something bad. Or were investors sitting in the cabin of the helicopter, planning to develop the bay into a resort? No, the bay was a nature reserve, there were no investors sitting in the helicopter, rather agents or mafiosi, in suits or leather jackets, with laptops or pistols or both. Should I warn Irene? Would I even be able to find her?

I sensed that I was no longer alone on the veranda. I looked around; the boy was standing a couple of feet away, the one who had squatted on the balcony two nights ago, his dark, deep eyes trained on me: Kari. His facial features looked so strange that I couldn't guess his age. Older than eighteen at any rate, old enough to warn Irene.

"Can you find Irene?"

"What do they want?"

"I don't know. But she should know that the helicopter was here."

He nodded, turned around and ran away – swift, smooth, effortless. I watched and listened to him go until he disappeared into the trees on the mountain. For a moment, it was quiet. Again I heard the waves rustle back through the pebbles into the sea. I closed my eyes against the sun.

Then the helicopter came back. First I heard it, then I saw it. It flew towards the old house, where I stood under the roof, hung in the air, sank and set down on the jetty. Again it churned up the sea. Then the motor died, and the helicopter let its rotor blades hang down. The pilot descended and helped the passenger out. An old, gaunt man with a cane, but with full, white hair, an upright posture, and confident movements. Gundlach.

# 12

"Did Schwind send you? Are you representing him again? He wants the painting, doesn't he?" He came towards me, full of energy, using his cane but talking all the while. Then he was standing right in front of me.

He annoyed me. I hadn't liked him when I visited his house and he took my arm. I had always found him condescending when we ran into each other on social occasions, and now I found him rude. "Didn't you give him the painting? And in return he gave you Irene? Who you couldn't keep?"

He snorted scornfully. "That was all juvenile nonsense. The painting is mine. It was gone, now it's back. Has your client . . ."

"Schwind is not my client."

"So what are you doing here?"

"Is that any of your business?"

He waved the question away. "You were always hypersensitive. Amazing that you succeeded as a lawyer. When will Irene be back?"

I shrugged.

"Then I'll take a look around. She's found a pretty spot for herself, no one comes, no one disturbs her, and for all that, it doesn't even belong to her. I'd have to work hard for something like this."

He took a few steps, then turned back and scrutinized me. "You, here . . ." He shook his head. "I always suspected you, but I didn't want to believe that as an attorney you would have dared." Then he laughed. "In any case, you had a good eye, better than mine. If I had suspected that the painting would one day be worth more than twenty million . . ."

I watched him wander off, going inside the lower house, re-emerging, climbing the steps to the upper house and disappearing inside. He tapped his cane hard on the steps and then on the floorboards; for a while after he had disappeared from sight, I heard the click-clack of his cane. Then it was quiet. The pilot sat on the edge of the jetty, dangling his legs and smoking a cigarette.

# 13

I went to meet Irene, following the tracks that led towards the farms as best I could. Then I sat down on a stone and waited. The air was again filled with the scent of pine and eucalyptus, and the chirr of cicadas. Despite the rain the day before, everything was dry, the grass and brush were brown, and the trees stretched parched branches towards the sky. From far away, I heard the Jeep.

Irene looked exhausted again. I told her that Gundlach was here; she wasn't upset, as I had expected, but animated; her eyes shone, colour came into her cheeks, her voice became strong. She wanted to know what he and I had talked about, and I told her. "Yes," she said laughing, "that's how he is."

"You expected him?"

She nodded.

"You gave the painting to the gallery to lure him here?"

She shrugged her shoulders – evasive, agreeing, rejecting, maybe annoyed at the "lure".

"Is Schwind coming too?"

"I hope so."

"When you gave the painting to the gallery, did you think about me too?"

"Did I want to lure you here too? I wanted to see Peter

and Karl again. I wasn't thinking of you."

I knew that I had no right to be, but I was hurt. Despite the rough road, she noticed, and laid her hand on my arm. I put it back. "You need both hands to drive."

"I want to know what's left. And back then, was I really just a trophy and a muse? What were they for me? I think I must have loved how uncompromising they were, the relentless energy with which Peter got richer and richer, and ever more powerful, and how Karl tried to paint the perfect work of art. They were both obsessed, and I was looking for something that would take possession of me. I'd come into an inheritance, my mother let me do what I wanted, on the condition that I let her do what she wanted. I studied art history, worked in the museum and thought . . . I really thought that with the right man I'd find the right life. A life where something great would possess me, something I wanted to give everything for."

Why had she never had children, but rather gathered children off the street? Instead, I asked what she expected to be left. "That Gundlach still wants to be richer and more powerful? That Schwind still wants to paint the perfect picture?"

She stopped. "I don't know."

"That they still love you?"

"That would be silly." She went silent, then spoke again slowly and hesitantly. "I would be happy enough if I recognized them. And could remember why I loved them. Why I left them. You had a steady life. Mine feels like a vase that fell to the floor and shattered into pieces."

# 14

Irene and Gundlach greeted each other with a hug. They showered each other with questions until they laughed, realizing that they were too many and too big. The simple ones remained. Was he sleeping here? The pilot too? Were they hungry? Gundlach offered to have dinner flown in, but was also happy with anything that Irene might serve. While Irene and I cooked, he stood next to us, propped up on his cane, and told us about the article in the New York Times and the reports that followed in the German media. The painting, Woman on Staircase, a fixture in Schwind catalogues, but never exhibited, about which Schwind had always been evasive, had a mysterious aura, and its sudden appearance in, of all places, the Art Gallery of New South Wales was a sensation.

Gundlach called the pilot in to eat, then sent him away. He would have liked to send me away too. While Irene was putting candles and red wine on the table, he asked: "Can we talk in private?" She smiled and said: "I have no secrets from him." It made me happy, even if it wasn't true.

Gundlach talked about his successes and his children, about his worries for the future of the company and the country, about his pride in his life's work. I didn't hear obsession, but the self-satisfied balance sheet of a self-satisfied, upstanding citizen. As she had with me, Irene turned his questions into questions of her own, giving nothing away about herself. It did not seem to disturb him. I asked myself if, like me, he was too polite to show his irritation, or if he didn't insist because he already knew what he wanted to know about her. He smiled each time she deflected a question.

Then he spoke of his marriage. He was happy, his wife was a good woman, a successful realtor, yet always there for him when he needed her. But she was so young that he often felt old. He looked at Irene. "You were young too, but with you I never felt old. I know, I was younger, the age gap was smaller. But that wasn't all. Seeing you in the painting just now, I felt young again." He smiled. "Paintings halt the march of time. I had you painted back then so you would stay young, and I with you." Gundlach leant forwards and took Irene's hand. "I did everything wrong back then. You couldn't live with me. But let me have your painting."

Irene looked out at the sea. Her face had lost all freshness and colour, only weariness and exhaustion remained. The break from her illness, which she didn't want to talk about, was over. She ran her hand over Gundlach's head, the way you'd pet a dog that came and sat next to you, and stood up. She could barely stay on her feet, but when I wanted to get up and help her, she gave me a look that forbade it. She didn't want to seem weak in front of Gundlach. "Good night." She walked slowly to the stairs and up them; at each step she paused to gather her strength for the next step, and for another, and yet another. I found it painful to watch.

"What's wrong with her?" whispered Gundlach.

"Ask her yourself." Then I couldn't hold back. "You really laid it on thick. Amazing that you've been so successful in business and politics. I thought one needed a certain sensitivity for that."

"The way you see people is too simplistic. The soul of a poet and the brains of a merchant – I don't wish to compare myself with Rathenau, but the two are compatible. There's nothing contradictory about wanting to live with the painting while enjoying the money that's rightfully mine."

"You've read Rathenau?"

"Yes. And Weber and Schumpeter and Marx. If those names mean anything to you. I have more than accounts and stocks in my head. And if I'm right and you helped Irene back then, and I bring that up in court, you're finished as an attorney. You should pray that I don't have to take anyone to court to get the painting, not Schwind and not Irene."

He had become ever louder. I asked him to calm down; Irene wanted to sleep.

"There's no reason she shouldn't hear what I have to say. Everyone here seems to know everything anyway; I can't talk to Irene without you sitting next to us. Take a walk tomorrow, a nice long walk. Do you understand me?"

While I was wondering whether I should nod simply to calm Gundlach down, Kari stepped out from the dark. He did nothing threatening, yet there was a menace in his presence. He looked at Gundlach and raised his finger to his mouth. Gundlach stared back at Kari as if he'd seen a ghost. Then Kari disappeared, and Gundlach took a deep breath. He shook his head. "I . . . I'm going to bed."

# 15

Irene did not get up the next morning. I was woken by the click-clack of Gundlach's cane on the stairs. I got dressed, went to the window and saw him standing by the beach, staring out at the sea. The pilot must have got up and left the house quietly. He was back on the jetty, dangling his legs and smoking.

Had Irene called? I knocked on her door, and she said "Come in" weakly. She was lying in bed, her head on a pillow propped against the wall, and she looked so bad – her face pale, her cheeks sunken, her hair soaked in sweat – that I would have liked to fly her straight to hospital in the helicopter. I sat on the edge of the bed and took her hand.

"What's wrong with you?"

She shook her head.

"You have no secrets from me."

She smiled. "Only a couple."

"With the helicopter, it's . . ."

"I'll be all right in a minute. Can you bring a strong coffee?"

Whatever I did would be wrong. Carrying her against her will to the helicopter and flying her to hospital would be wrong. Helping her, pumping her up with coffee, so she could run around all day and be exhausted again by evening, would be wrong. Her lying in bed, with me looking after her until she felt better: she wouldn't want that. Not looking after her as she lay in bed: I simply couldn't do that.

"And if Karl comes today? I can rest when Peter and Karl have gone, tomorrow or the day after. Now, I need to get up. Help me? Please?"

So I made a strong coffee, brought her the pot and a cup in bed, and I fetched a leather bag from the wardrobe, from which she took a small mirror, some white powder, a razor blade and a glass tube. I watched her snort cocaine. She needed support on her way to the bathroom; after that, she managed without my help. When she emerged from the bathroom, her stride was heavy but firm, her eyes animated. She was lively, as she had been after Gundlach's arrival the day before.

"It's already late. I'll make breakfast. Will you find the others?"

On the way to the beach I saw the boat round the edge of the cove and by the time I reached Gundlach, he had seen it too. The boat came closer. A figure was standing in front of the small cabin, Schwind, and as he grew clearer to us, so must we have grown clearer to him. Schwind and Gundlach had time to prepare for each other. I wished the both of them would go to hell.

# 16

Schwind got off the same boat I had. He nodded to me and Gundlach, took stock of things, and marched decisively off to the house on the hillside. He was bald, massive, radiating strength.

When Gundlach and I entered the kitchen, Schwind was holding Irene in his arms. "Where were you? I looked for you, I've always looked for you." Then he saw us, let Irene go, went to the door, grabbed it and barked: "Out!"

Irene laughed. "Everyone sit down. Breakfast's almost ready." She seemed to be enjoying it all: Schwind's embrace, his outburst, the tension in the room.

"What are we still doing here? Let's go, the boat is waiting. We can have breakfast in Rock Harbour, then take the night flight from Sydney to New York. I've spoken with the gallery. One word from you, and they'll send the painting to New York in time for the retrospective. Remember how we dreamed of that? An exhibition in the MoMA?"

Irene nodded.

"We dreamed of the opening, the toasts, the admiration of the guests, the praise of the critics. We dreamed of the walk through Central Park back to the hotel, the champagne, the huge bathtub, the king-sized bed with the view of the city. It's finally happening."

Irene's smile was friendly, amused, distant. "Sounds nice."

Gundlach couldn't take any more. "Nonsense! You had your first big exhibition in New York years ago. You might have dreamed about that once. But you don't dream about the retrospective that already showed in Berlin and Tokyo and now comes to New York! Do you even have dreams any more? A colleague described you as a calculating mind that manipulates the public, the market, your own prices. I'm a businessman, I have no problem with that. But don't tell Irene fairy tales!"

Schwind saw only Irene. He looked at her with the child-like, confident gaze I recognized. "You've never been to an exhibition of mine – not the painting, not you. New York next week – it would be the first exhibition where every-thing is as it should be."

"It would be the first exhibition where everything is as it should be," Gundlach parroted. "All you want is the painting."

"What is he talking about?" Schwind looked at Irene as if they were listening to an idiot blather. "I've talked to the curator and explained that you've watched over my painting for a long time, and that I understand that he can't send it to New York without your say-so. What does that have to do with him?" He nodded in Gundlach's direction.

Before Gundlach could explain, Irene reminded everyone about breakfast. "The coffee's hot, the bacon's getting cold, the eggs need to go in the pan." She said to me: "Can you fetch the pilot? And can you ask Mark if he'll come up for a coffee?"

# 17

By the time I came back with the two of them, a ceasefire was in effect. Gundlach did not interrupt Schwind while he told Irene about his abstract works, and Schwind didn't interrupt Gundlach while he talked about business succession planning. Irene reigned over them like a queen, and over us: the pilot, Mark, and me as we talked of the first and last cigarettes in our lives. I hadn't seen her so lively, so effervescent, so beautiful since I had arrived. How long could a cocaine high last?

After breakfast, Mark went back in the boat. Irene or I would take Schwind to Rock Harbour when the time came. The pilot offered to fly him, but Gundlach snapped at him that he had hired the helicopter and needed it to be kept ready, the pilot should go and make sure that the thing would fly when needed.

Then Gundlach looked around the group. "Let's talk about this reasonably. I'm the last authenticated owner of the painting. To claim it as yours, Schwind, you would have to have received it from me in some way – how? On the basis of the contract? The contract was worthless. Indeed, where is it? In any case, you surely don't want to call on the contract in court and then read in the press that you traded your lover for the painting, because it was worth more to you than her."

"The press eats out of my hand. I'll give them a version of the story that leaves you looking like the bad guy, not me. The contract was unenforceable, I know that now, but if you make an unenforceable contract, you're not entitled to get back what you gave to fulfill your end of it. You gave the painting to me in the house."

"Gave? The painting was still on my property, still in the hands of my butler, and had yet to enter your possession. That never happened; the vehicle in which the painting was placed was not in your possession, but rather that of the thief – the lady thief, as we now know, and her accomplice."

"If you thought the painting still belonged to you, why didn't you report the loss? Why isn't the picture on the register of stolen art?"

"Why didn't I report the loss? I suspected even then that Irene stole the painting. I didn't want to harm her."

"How would registering the painting harm her? And if you didn't want to harm Irene then, why do you want to do it now?"

"I don't want to hurt her. All she needs to do is to make it clear to the gallery that it's my painting. In fact, there's no reason it shouldn't stay on display at the art gallery. Or you could show it at your retrospective as a loan." Gundlach turned to Irene. "But you have to put an end to this."

He gave her a pained look, and suddenly I realized what this was about. Yes, the painting and the money, but something else was more important. Gundlach felt inferior to Irene, as inferior as he had back then, when she left him and he couldn't win her back. Perhaps he hadn't ever felt equal to her – a woman who had never given up her resistance, refusal, and spite. Irene was the defeat of his life, and he had to compensate for that defeat.

Then he laughed. It was an ugly, mocking laugh. "So from the beginning. If he," Gundlach nodded in my direction, "still has the contract, he'll never dig it up. That's not the sort of contract you draw up, not even as a young lawyer, and as an old one you'd rather you'd never drawn it up. No, Schwind, the contract is of no use to you. If you're thinking that you have Irene as a witness – Irene won't help you either. You won't testify in court as a witness, Irene."

"You're right, I won't go to court." She stood up. "The painting . . ."

But Gundlach wouldn't be deprived of his triumph. "The police are looking for you in Germany. They'll look for you in Australia if they know you're here. I don't know how no one recognized you. Because you were never arrested, never booked. So the police didn't have a good mugshot, just a photo from a speed camera with you in sunglasses, with dyed hair, with your head down? But I recognized you from the wanted poster, and if you go back into the world, others will recognize you too."

# 18

Irene didn't reply. She looked at Gundlach doubtfully, as if she didn't know what to make of his revelations, or of him, or of herself. Then she shrugged and smiled. "Do you want to turn me in?"

"What did you do back then? You knew our routines, how we lived, where we drove – your friends could have put you to good use."

"We?" Irene gave Gundlach a mocking look.

"I know you. Your spite, your antagonism, your rebelliousness. You didn't just want to hurt me, and him," he turned his head towards Schwind, "and him," and towards me, "you wanted to get even with everyone. How far did you go? Did you want to knock on the door one day as if everything was back to normal? And shoot Hannes first, and then me?" Gundlach was talking himself into a rage. "Hannes liked you, he was my butler, but he liked you more than me. Of course he would have let you in and it would have been easy for you . . . him then me . . . or me first and then him . . ." Gundlach was looking at Irene as if she were threatening him even now.

"You think I wanted to shoot you?"

"If you didn't, then your friends would have wanted to,

with your help. You think I don't remember? I remember everything, how you hated our lifestyle, your dream of throwing yourself into some grand cause. To be on the cutting edge of history – do you remember? And when I asked you what you would have done with this idea under Hitler or Stalin, you looked at me defiantly and had nothing to say. Then you thought the artist would be the thing, and then the revolution. Killing the man you'd abandoned anyway – that's not too much to ask in the name of revolution!"

"No one wanted to kill you. No one thought you were that important."

Gundlach leapt to his feet. He propped his hands on the table, leant down to Irene and barked at her. "And if your friends had thought I was important enough? What then? Would you have joined in? Would you have pulled the trigger?"

I am always slow to respond, but Schwind too did nothing, and just watched. Kari intervened. Wherever he had been, he had heard Gundlach getting angry and imagined that Irene was in danger. He had quietly slipped behind Gundlach. He took him by his upper arms and sat him back down in his chair. Gundlach was ashen, trembling and struggling for air – I don't know what a heart attack looks like, but that is how I imagine one.

Irene stood up, went to Gundlach, took his hand, took his pulse and shook her head: nothing. She wrapped her arms around him.

# 19

No one wanted to speak. Schwind's brow was furrowed as he watched Irene hold Gundlach in her arms. The sea washed through the pebbles, and a bird sang four notes, over and over.

"I would never have done anything to you. As crazy as life was, as crazy as I was . . ." Irene shook her head. "I'd gone to pieces, freed from all confines – and everything that had held me together. Life felt like a drug. Afterwards, it was like I was in withdrawal, with sleepless nights, my heart racing, breaking out into sweats. But that passed too, and then all that remained was this enormous emptiness: everything was far away, colours were dull, sounds were weak, I couldn't feel anything any more. Except anger. I hadn't known that I could get so angry, screaming, pounding tables with my fists, punching walls and then weeping, weeping from anger . . ."

She let go of Gundlach, who had pulled himself together, and looked at us, one by one. She saw our bewilderment at her sudden confession. She sat down and laughed. "You know, the colours in East Germany were duller than in the West. The plaster was gray-brown, like Brandenburg sand, the old stone buildings were never cleaned, the Reichsbahn trains were a worn-out shade of green, the flags and banners a faded red. But life there saved me. After the crazy years, it was like a stay in a sanatorium, where there was little to be had but peace and quiet. No colours to catch your eye, no music to get under your skin, no erotic promises on every billboard, no bargains to be hunted. And in the sanatorium nothing changes, not really, and life goes on the same way, day in, day out."

Gundlach waved his hand dismissively, as if shooing something away. "You aren't seriously trying to tell us—"

"I'm not trying to paint a false picture. The nanny state, the inefficiencies, the shortages – that's all true. But I didn't suffer. It was . . . it was like staying with the Amish. The Amish can leave – which wasn't possible there – but their life is strict and austere, like mine was, and I didn't want to leave. The way time stood still, the peace and quiet, the absence of sensations – it did me good. Celebrating finishing the dacha after all the effort and cunning required to scrape together the materials, and all the work your friends and family had put in; going to the opera in Berlin with your colleagues; canoeing and camping in the Spreewald; reading the classics, which were easy to get hold of, and the other books, which weren't – that was enough for me."

Schwind laughed mockingly. "A Biedermeier paradise?"

"Maybe that's not a bad comparison. There was no political freedom in the Biedermeier period either."

"But beautiful furniture, trips to France, and if you'd had enough, you could go to America."

"I don't need beautiful furniture. I don't need to travel, not unless I need to. I loved the countryside, the lightness around Saale and Unstrut, the melancholy of Mecklenburg and Pomerania, even the bleakness of the strip mines. I loved the mild summer rain in Bitterfeld, a mist of damp and smoke and chemicals. And the spring rain that pours down the worn-out streets and washes winter dirt from the cracks and potholes. I loved the trams, they were run-down, but they were allowed to just be trams, and not billboards for Coca-Cola and long legs."

"The grime over there was no better than the pomp and bombast of the Nazis." Gundlach was indignant. "There are political truths."

"I lived with a painter. Wherever you are, there is more to daily life than happiness and unhappiness, justice and injustice. There's beauty. Ugliness too, but I took pleasure in the beauty that was there and is now gone for ever."

"Why didn't you stay there?"

"You know why. After 1990, there was no more 'there'. All there was *was* 'here' and the photo of the woman with sunglasses and dyed hair."

"Why didn't they catch you?"

"Like the others? Because I left as soon as the Wall fell. I had my old things at my mother's, I had my old passport, issued in 1980 and valid until 1990, just long enough to make it here. They never looked for me under my real name, until the Wall fell they just had my photo and the name I had lived under in the East." She got up. "I need to lie down, I hope you don't mind. Shall we see each other at five for an aperitif and then eat together? Will you have dinner flown in today, as you offered yesterday? Can you help me up the stairs?"

# 20

I helped her up the stairs and into bed. After looking in her leather bag, I could reassure her: she had enough cocaine for tonight and tomorrow morning and beyond. She was asleep before I left the room.

I remembered the wanted posters that hung in government buildings and post offices and were shown after the television news. I never took a close look. Under the label "Terrorists" – Irene? With sunglasses, dyed hair, her head bowed? Wanted for involvement in murder, criminal use of explosives, and bank robbery? With a warning that she was armed and dangerous? With the promise of a reward? No, I didn't remember that.

My wife had a hard time with faces; prosopagnosia is, as I have since learned, a cognitive disposition like dyslexia or dyscalculia. One struggles to identify faces and also to recognize them again. It's a terrible handicap for a politician; it cost my wife a great deal of energy and discipline not to upset the people she dealt with in local politics. Because she hadn't realized that it was a cognitive disorder, she had blamed herself and thought she was a bad person who didn't pay enough attention to her fellow human beings. I never had a problem with faces.

I couldn't find Schwind and Gundlach in the kitchen, nor on the balcony. Then I heard their voices on the beach, but they were hard to make out. They must have been sitting on the bench on the veranda.

They were no longer arguing. It sounded as if they were licking their wounds. Was Irene the great defeat of Schwind's life, as she had been of Gundlach's? Had he imagined then that he could have both – the painting, because Schwind owed it to him, and Irene, because she belonged to him? And then Irene had robbed him of both, had taken the painting from him and then left, herself?

I thought of my grandfather, who would sometimes say that he had dreamed of his finals at school again. At the time I couldn't believe that an early experience, which had been followed by a long, full life, could remain so present. My grandfather had passed his finals without any difficulty, studied medicine, opened a practice and run it successfully. And still he dreamed about his finals? Schwind was the world's most famous, expensive contemporary painter, idolized by students, courted by critics, desired by women – and still he suffered over some trivial setback from decades ago? And Gundlach, a man who was successful several times over, worth millions, father of two adult children, happily married, couldn't come to terms with the fact that this defiant woman had left him so long ago?

Or is it the small defeats that we can't get over? The first tiny scratch on a new car is more painful than a big one later on. The small splinters are harder to remove than the big ones and sometimes won't come out however much you poke them with a needle, and they fester until they work their way out. The big early defeats change the course of our lives. The small ones don't change us, but they stay with us and torment us, little thorns in our side.

Then there seems to be a chance to put things right; it seems so close that you reach out and try to take it, but then it's all smoke and mirrors. I was starting to understand Gundlach and Schwind. Not that I felt a connection with them. My experience with Irene had nothing in common with theirs.

# 21

When I went to join them on the beach, they were talking about their children and grandchildren. How many they had, how they were getting on in life, whose children and grandchildren were more successful — for a fraction of a second I was tempted to join them and boast about my own children and grandchildren.

I asked Schwind something I had been wondering about since his arrival. "Did you really reserve the right to decide what happened to all your paintings, whom they could be sold or lent to?"

"What?" He looked at me blankly.

"You said to me then that you would never let what happened to Irene's painting happen to another painting of yours. That all your paintings would remain under . . ."

He shook his head. "Did I say that? That sounds more like the sort of thing you'd say, something you'd write in one of your little legal notebooks. I don't need to have control over my paintings." He chuckled. "It's enough that they have control over the viewer."

Gundlach joined in with a contemptuous laugh.

I didn't know whether the object of Gundlach's scorn was me or Schwind. I didn't want to let him annoy me. "It's one o'clock, and we're meeting at five for an aperitif. Don't you want to dispatch your pilot?"

Gundlach waved his hand dismissively. "Do you want to take care of dinner? He should put it on my tab at the hotel."

So I went. We flew along the coast with the sea below us, little waves with white crests, which gleamed in the sun and were dull in the shade. To the right there was rock and sand, green and brown land, towns and roads. We could see Sydney from a long way away; the city sprawled up the coast. The flight was loud, despite the headphones with ear protectors, but after our talk over breakfast about our first and last cigarettes, we had nothing else to talk about. Anyway, I preferred to look down. Everything looked cozy from up here: the houses, the gardens, the cars, the parks, the beaches, the yachts with their colourful, billowing sails, the people. Then we flew over the sights of Sydney – Harbour Bridge, the Opera House, the Botanic Garden. People were lying in the grass on the big lawn next to the Conservatory. I could have been one of them.

We didn't land on the roof of a skyscraper, as I had imagined, but at the outer edge of the airport. In the taxi, it came out that the pilot loved cooking, and he told me all about barramundi, crocodile and kangaroo, about Australian desserts, the country's grape varieties, its wine-growing regions. He put together our evening menu enthusiastically. Caviar, barramundi with shiitake, kangaroo with macadamia nuts, passion fruit pavlova with Granny Smith sorbet as a palate cleanser between courses, with champagne, Sauvignon Blanc, and an assemblage of Cabernet Sauvignon, Merlot and Shiraz. Anything we couldn't have prepared, because it would get cold, he'd finish in Irene's kitchen – it all sounded fine to me. I left him negotiating with the chef, went and sat on the hotel terrace and watched the harbour.

I needed to call. Even if my children wouldn't be worried about me, and most probably hadn't even thought about me, they should at least know where I was. It was between five and six in Europe, too early to wake them. In our family, we did, and still do things by the book: no loud fights, no love fests or orgies of joy, no lazing about, as much work as possible, as much rest as necessary; day is day and night is night. The kids should sleep. But I could call the firm's manager; he has to work for the firm even when he's at home.

He was as awake as if it were the middle of the day. "Are you ill? You still don't know when you can fly? The doctor says there's no cause for alarm? You're hard to get hold of." The connection was bad, and his questions reassured him that he had understood me correctly. "Call your children?" He was ready to take care of that too and was certain he could give me my colleagues' regards in return for mine.

I turned off the phone. I never had, nor wanted a boat; the sea and new shores and foreign ports had never tempted me. But now I had the happy feeling that with that call, I'd cut the line that kept my boat moored.

# 22

The pilot took over the kitchen. The mushrooms and nuts only needed to be warmed up, the barramundi and kangaroo had to be cooked. I set the table on the balcony, dressed the caviar with sour cream, lemon, onions and eggs, and found a jug that would do as a bucket, in which I placed the champagne with ice from the hotel cooler. On the way from the hotel to the airport I had bought a bouquet of roses, red, yellow and white. I put on my new linen trousers and a new shirt, and as I stood on the balcony at quarter past five, Gundlach and Schwind arrived, one from one direction, the other from the other.

Then Irene came. She hadn't asked for my help, and I hadn't offered it; this was her night, her time to shine. She walked serenely onto the balcony, wearing a black top and a long black skirt. She wore her hair up, and lipstick, and a necklace of gray pearls wound twice around her neck. She was radiant and smiling, basking in our admiration. She let Gundlach pass her a glass, let me pour, and let Schwind fix a white rose to her top with a safety pin he conjured up from his pocket. The roe were like pearls, the barramundi juicy, the kangaroo tender, and the conversation skated over trivial things.

Until I asked Irene: "Do you know now? What's left from those days? Do you see what you once saw in them? And why you left them?"

I couldn't tell how Irene looked at me. Like I'd woken her from a dream? Like she couldn't believe I'd interjected something? Gundlach and Schwind were clearly taken aback, and I understood why; I had said almost nothing since they arrived.

"Oh, yes. I recognize Karl's feet, the big, strong feet he stands on, steady in the world. I recognize his bluster and his confidence, and remember believing I'd be protected between those two pillars. I recognize Peter's will and strength, and now that he needs a cane, the cane sounds like his steps did back then, when he'd get his cobbler to nail iron caps to the soles of his shoes. I remember how ambitious they both were. Back then I often felt too young for them, like their daughter instead of their partner. Now I feel almost like their mother. I can see that they've made their way in the world and been successful, and I'm happy for them. And when I left them, it was the right thing to do. When the children grow up, the mother has to go."

"The mother?"

Irene's look begged me to say no more, to ask no skeptical questions that would challenge this new role, mother, which she'd traded for the old ones of trophy and muse. Did she just want to look beautiful and be admired, and enjoy the evening?

"You didn't leave us because you wanted to send your children out into the world. You didn't lure us here in order to reminisce about his feet, and my shoes. What did he ask?" Gundlach looked in my direction. "What's left? Did you

139

really want to know what was left from our years together? From your time with him?" Now he tipped his head towards Schwind. "It was just an interlude. Nothing more. It happened by chance. If you hadn't been in the Arts and Crafts Museum the day my Japanese guests wanted a tour and the tour guide was missing – and if the other painter hadn't gone to Rome and I hadn't had to hire this one," again, he meant Schwind, "and if he," he jabbed his chin at me, "hadn't made a mess of everything . . . The interlude started by chance, it ended by chance, it's all a long time ago. Life went on."

"Is that how you see your whole life? As a series of interludes?"

The question took Gundlach by surprise. He gave Schwind a searching look, then decided that his interest was genuine. "Of course not. My father turned a workshop into a factory and I built the factory into a thriving business. My life had a purpose. The encounters that don't change life's course or goal may be as beautiful as you wish, but they're still interludes."

"Your wives, your children, your grandchildren . . ."

"They are part of the goal. What I've built should last – the same goes for you. You see, at sixteen I had to help shoot down war planes. I started off at Deutsche Bank as a trainee and finished as the chairman's assistant, I took over the factory during the first oil crisis, I was already in America before reunification, and since then I've been in Eastern Europe and China as well. We don't need to grow. But although our world isn't changing, it's still in motion, and if we want to keep our place, we need to keep moving too. Whether my children and grandchildren can manage it . . .

140

The gene pool of a family business is limited."

"The End of History?" Schwind asked.

"History goes on. But our world doesn't change. Nothing threatens it now, no communism, no fascism, no young people who want to turn it upside down. Since the end of the Cold War there's no alternative to our world. Name one country that doesn't live under the laws of capitalism – even China's communism is capitalism now. The word of the prophet, for which the Muslims kill and die, is no alternative – it's a task for the police and the military. You worry about the poor? As long as they have TV, and beer on the table, they're no threat. And we can always give them that."

# 23

"That sounds . . ." Schwind searched for the right word. "Leaden."

"Is your art leaden?" Gundlach asked. "I don't know much about art, but after we met . . ."

"After our interlude?" Schwind said ironically.

"Interlude, exactly, after which I followed your career, how you got famous and expensive. Representation, abstraction, photography as material, glass as object and image, the structures and the colours – you played with everything, like a child, who, sits amidst his older siblings' games picking up one toy from one, another from the other. Everything is available to you, and you make use of everything. And there is no longer any alternative to your art."

Irene turned to Schwind. "Is that who you are?"

Before Schwind could respond, Gundlach went on. "I'm almost done. That is who you are, because the world no longer changes. It continues to move, but the movements in business and finance and culture and politics are all repetitions, they no longer change the world. Your art is in motion too, sometimes in one and the same work. That's why it's beautiful. But it changes nothing." He became earnest. "Yes, I want Irene's painting back home with me."

"What's art supposed to change? I painted what I saw. Sometimes I saw things that weren't there, but could have been there, and painted those too. I painted as well as I could. That's all."

"I know. You didn't set out to make art for which there was no alternative. But you couldn't make anything else: nobody can, with the world and art being what they are: reliable, manageable, without alternative. One can put on a gag or trigger a scandal. But that too is just always same old, same old."

"What will finally melt the lead?"

"I don't know. A nuclear war? A meteor strike? Some other catastrophe that brings the end of the world as we know it? But I don't find the world leaden. I like it how it is, and you like it too. It is how it always was before communism and fascism tore everything apart. There are the rich, and everybody else; the rich take care of things and everybody else makes do."

"Take care?"

Gundlach laughed. "Take care that nothing changes."

I looked at Irene and started to worry. The effects of the cocaine were wearing off. Her face betrayed her exhaustion and despair as the illness regained its grip. She saw my gaze, her expression turned defiant, and she stood up. With heavy legs she walked to the stairs, then upstairs.

"I remember the women," Schwind was back in the hopes and dreams of the late sixties and early seventies. "The beautiful, clever women from good backgrounds who went over to the left out of political conviction, and because they could sense it was where the avant-garde was, where life was exciting. Before I met Irene with you, I saw her at a debate at the university. All she did was sit and listen, but the way she sat and listened – it was clear that this was where the future was being negotiated."

"The future?" Gundlach asked scornfully.

The pilot came, we cleared the table, brought out dessert, then washed up. I kept my ear to the stairs all the while. Once we were finished in the kitchen, the pilot took a bottle of red wine and left. I watched him go down to the jetty, sit down, and drink and smoke. His cigarette glowed in the dark.

# 24

Then Irene came down the stairs. Had she been waiting for the dark? When I wanted to take two candles out onto the balcony, she signalled that one was enough.

I hadn't followed Gundlach and Schwind's conversation. It had briefly grown loud, then quieted again. As Irene sat down, Gundlach said: "You still haven't told us what you did in those days."

"If I killed someone? Is that what you mean? I was part of it. I still didn't know that nothing would change. No one knew. We thought: if there was a West and an East, then there could also be something else, better than both. Now that neither world exists any more, I understand what you're saying. Perhaps I already understood it when I lived in East Germany. It was finished. Exhausted by the ideological excesses, the empty rituals, the efforts that had come to nothing."

"Why so sad?"

"Do you guys know the feeling? That, when it comes to it, not only will you die, the whole world will end with you? You might think that once you're dead, it doesn't make a difference if the world goes on or ends. But it does."

Gundlach had no interest in the death of the individual

and the end of the world. "How do you live here illegally?"

"It's not hard if you have money in the bank in Germany, if you pay with a credit card and get cash advances from it, and don't need the state. Bringing the painting here wasn't quite so easy. Who travels with luggage like that?"

Schwind had been listening to Gundlach and Irene with visible impatience. "The end of the world, the end of East Germany – all well and good. Can someone finally tell me how I get my painting back? My painting – I painted it, I fixed it when he damaged it," Schwind pointed at Gundlach, "paid for it . . ."

"Paid for it?" Gundlach was outraged. "You had had enough of Irene and brought her to me – you call that paying? I know why you want the painting – you never painted like that again. Ever since then you've been recycling the history of art."

"I am—"

"You are a burned-out painter who weeps for beginnings. Go cry elsewhere. You have no claim to make here, neither moral nor legal. You have no right to the painting, which you sold, and no right to Irene, whom you betrayed. Pack your bags, and let him," he tipped his head in my direction, "take you back."

"What an arrogant ass you are! All because of your money, that couldn't buy you the woman or even the painting? You accumulated it as thoughtlessly as you'd collect beer coasters. You are a coaster collector, and the world without alternatives you talked about is the world of beer coasters. Don't you get it? Money can't buy you the things that matter!"

"Ha!" Gundlach laughed derisively. "The court painter of global capitalism reveals himself as a critic of capitalism.

146

Why do you sell your pictures for millions? Why don't you just donate them?"

Irene wanted to say something, but couldn't get a word in, so I tried to break up the argument. "Can the two of you—"

"Our lawyer!" Gundlach stopped me. "He," he nodded his head at Schwind, "has at least created an *oeuvre* and made a fortune with it, and I did what I did, but you? Fancy firm, I know, big cases, but always doing other people's dirty work – you are a lackey, sir. First you were his," again he tipped his head towards Schwind, "then mine, then hers." Then, to Irene, "You'd do best to keep quiet."

"What the hell—" I wasn't going to take that lying down.

"A lackey." Schwind laughed, loudly. "A lackey. Like the butlers, who think they're a cut above, but they're still just lackeys. I remember your butler. A servile soul, who—"

"He was a better man than you. He never said it out loud, but he missed the painting too, and I feel bad that he can't see it in its old place. Irene," he spoke with the friendly patience one uses with a fractious child, "I want to leave you in peace, no police, no criminal trial, no lawsuit for the painting either. We can't put everything right that went wrong back then. But the painting needs to go back where it belongs."

"Same old tune!" Schwind threw up his hands, fingers splayed, then let them sink down again as he had back in my office. "Everything has a place, where it belongs, and when it isn't where it belongs – stop it, Gundlach. It's enough. Irene ought to decide, and that should be the end of it. If she gives you the painting, then you should have it, and if she—"

Gundlach shook his head. "Irene only has one option, you know that as well as I. Ask our lackey. Ingratiating yourself with Irene won't help you and it doesn't help her."

"You were married to this asshole? This greedy—"

"Greedy? You want the painting as much as I do. You're not fooling anyone with your soft words, with your 'Irene should decide' – not me, not her."

Irene stood up. She looked awful, old, tired, ill. "I gave the painting to the Art Gallery weeks ago. It is no longer mine to give, to either of you. I just wanted to see you both again." She looked at me, and I laid my right arm around her and helped her to the stairs and then up the stairs. She lay down in bed without undressing, I pulled the blanket from underneath her and spread it on top of her. She was asleep when I shut the door.

# 25

When I came back down to the balcony, Gundlach and Schwind had found their voices again. "Can she give away something that doesn't belong to her?" Gundlach asked.

"You should have reported the painting to the register of stolen art," I said. "I'm certain that the Art Gallery contacted them and, since the painting wasn't registered with them, she is now the good-faith owner. If you want to know the legal details, ask your lackeys."

"All the drama with the loan just to lure us here? What did she want from us?" Gundlach shook his head. "Women! They don't understand that what's done is done. That if you want to move forwards you have to leave the past behind. Schlepping along old loves and friendships . . . you grow out of them like you grow out of old clothes. After a while they smell musty."

Gundlach may have been right, but he irritated me. "Didn't you want to stop the march of time? Didn't you want the painting back so you could stay young with the young Irene?"

"He said that?" Schwind asked.

"To stay young with the painting of the young Irene, I didn't need to come see the old one. Besides, you still haven't told us what you're doing here."

I stood up. "What does it matter?" I went down and sat on the beach and heard Gundlach and Schwind speculating as to why I was here. Then they recounted their futile journeys in funny little anecdotes, that they might tell at a party. Gundlach boasted about the Hans Gundlach Foundation, named for his father, which had paid for the restoration of village churches in Brandenburg and Mecklenburg. Schwind thought foundations were something for one's last will and testament, something for whatever was left after women and children, talked of his five children from four marriages, lamented the democratization and banalization of art, and mocked art therapy for the handicapped and painting contests for children.

I took off my shoes and socks. The sea was warm, I undressed and swam in the bright moonlight, until I could no longer hear the voices on the balcony and no longer see the light from the candle. At the end of the cove, a boulder rose up out of the water. Its slope was completely smooth, and I stretched out. The stone had absorbed the day's sun and warmed my back, and the balmy breeze stroked my face and chest and belly.

Had Irene wanted to be the same woman she had been for Gundlach and Schwind in those days? Her coquettishness in the role of mother, her pleasure at the pair's admiration, her laughter at their jokes, the sanitized story of her life – she had set out to please them. To draw them out? So she could see who they really were? Or was she still who she was back then to them, the way people say they're always children to their parents, even when they're adults and their parents are old?

It wasn't my business. I've got a sense for when something is or isn't, and I knew what was happening here was Irene, Gundlach, and Schwind's business, not mine. They could present themselves however they wanted; I was just a chance observer. I don't know why I suddenly felt guilty – not because I had helped Irene steal the painting back then, or because today I'd butted in to the game between her and the two men, or because my wife had driven the car into the tree, or because I hadn't seen my children in a long time. My children were adults, my wife had been too; I had mostly kept my mouth shut today and back then, done nothing that Irene couldn't have found others to do. My feeling of guilt wasn't about any one thing. It was like angst, although there was nothing to fear; sadness, although nothing had happened. It was a physical sensation, and although I said to myself that the body can only feel good or bad, but not guilty, it was a feeling of guilt. I was getting cold and swam back.

The house was dark and quiet. Kari was perched at the bottom of the stairs; we gave each other a nod, and I smiled at him, but he didn't smile back. There were still glasses and an open bottle of wine on the balcony, I poured myself some and sat down. Tomorrow, I could call my firm from Rock Harbour and have a colleague find out what the terrorist with dyed hair, sunglasses and a bowed head was accused of. But maybe Gundlach was right, and whatever Irene had done was part of a vanished world that had nothing in common with ours.

As I lay in bed I listened to the rush of the waves, and the rustle as they washed back through the pebbles. It was soft, I could barely hear it. I couldn't hear the house breathing either. There was a peculiar restlessness in the house, as if Irene couldn't keep her hands and legs still, as if Gundlach was tossing and turning in bed, as if Schwind was talking in his sleep and the pilot was pacing his room, smoking. As if the house were trembling, not shaken by the wind or a tremor, but under the burden of hosting incompatible people. I lay completely still.

# Part Three

# 1

The next morning the pilot knocked gently at the door and poked his head inside. Did I want to come along? Schwind would be coming too. They could take me all the way to Sydney, or drop me off in Rock Harbour. No? He waved and gently closed the door. I heard the three of them on the stairs, and then on the stairs down to the beach; they did not speak and they trod lightly. They're stealing away, I thought, but then I told myself that was a dumb idea. Then the engine roared to life, the rotor blades buzzed and rattled, the helicopter took off, grew quieter then louder again, as if circling around the beach and the house – and flew away. It had startled the birds; they flitted about, flapped their wings, warbled and cawed excitedly.

When at ten, Irene was still not up, I listened at her door, heard nothing, knocked, again heard nothing, and went in. It didn't just smell of sickness. It stank of excrement and urine despite the open window – a strong, pungent smell. Irene was lying in bed with her eyes open and looked at me, ashamed.

"Go. I'll get up in a minute. I just feel a little weak."

"Should I run a bath? Or do you want a shower?"

She started crying. "It's never happened before. I wanted

to get up and go to the bathroom, but I couldn't, and I was stuck lying down and I couldn't hold it."

"I'll get you in just a minute." I went into the bathroom, ran the tap, poured bath oil into the water, checked the temperature and adjusted the amount of foam. I waited for the bath to fill up. As a child, I liked having a bath; the tub was fed from a boiler on a stove, and I would flick water against the hot boiler and listen to it hiss. For decades, I've only taken showers. Having a bath is a waste of time. But Irene had time, and it would do her good to lie in the bath after her shower until I had her bed ready. We had time – we now had all the time in the world.

I picked her up; she lay an arm around my shoulder and let herself be half-carried, half-led to the bathroom. I undressed her in front of the shower and I washed her under the shower as she held fast to the handle. I had not changed my children and I had no idea how stubbornly dried-on excrement sticks to the skin. Once I'd cleaned Irene up, I lifted her into the tub. She kept her eyes closed throughout, and didn't say a word. I did not say anything either. I concentrated on getting her clean and keeping myself dry. I got wet anyway.

But I didn't want to get changed until I had sorted everything out. First I soaked the bed linen, then stuffed it, together with the pyjamas, into the propane washing machine. I carried Irene's mattress onto the balcony, washed it, and laid it in the sun, took a mattress from another room to her room and made her bed. I made tea and porridge and left them on the nightstand. Then I dried her off and carried her to bed; she again said nothing.

"I'll be back in a moment, I just want to get changed."

"The others have left?"

"Yes."

I stood in the door and stared at her until she smiled and said: "Don't look so serious!"

"What's wrong with you?"

"In a minute. Go get changed."

But when I came back to her room she had fallen asleep, and when she woke up she didn't want to talk about her health. She drank the lukewarm tea and ate the lukewarm porridge and wanted to be driven to the two farms, because she wanted Meredene to pick up some things in town, and because Meredene would have to start giving the man from the second farm his injections.

I wrapped Irene in a coat, buckled her tightly to the seat with a belt, and drove her to the farmsteads in the Jeep. When the trail vanished, she pointed out the way to me, and I tried to memorize the riverbeds, pools, clumps of trees and boulders that the trail led past. Next time, I might have to drive alone.

At both farms, Irene stayed in the Jeep. She had me fetch Meredene, and she explained to her that she would have to give the injections from now on, even if she preferred not to, and gave her the shopping list. "What about . . ." I began, and Irene knew what I wanted to say, and said: "Yes, I need diapers as well." At the other farm, the old woman grumpily took the news that Irene couldn't do it any more, and that in future Meredene would come in her stead, without a question or a word of thanks.

Irene watched her go. "I owe the house on the sea to her husband and I wanted to pay him back by looking after him until he passed away. Now he's going to survive me." She sensed my questioning look. "Pancreatic cancer. I've got a couple of weeks, maybe just one. I can't say for sure."

# 2

Irene wanted to lie on the balcony, rather than in her room. I went from room to room until I found a bed frame that was light to carry onto the balcony. The mattress I had washed was dry, and smelled of the sun.

"You should have left with the others," said Irene from the bed. "Now you have to stay until the end."

"Who diagnosed you?"

"The doctors at Sydney Cancer Centre."

"Did they say nothing more could be done?"

She laughed. "Believe me, if they could have done something, they'd have done it. That's how they make their living."

"Did you get a second opinion?"

"I got a second opinion, I looked into different treatments, I even researched miracle cures. And I'd rather you didn't interrogate me."

I was stung, because I had meant well, and annoyed with myself because I'd put it so clumsily. Irene noticed and said: "I know. If I could . . . I'd rather not die."

For the first time, it really hit me. Irene was going to die. Last year, on holiday, a colleague from the firm lost his strength, and appetite, and upon his return went to the doctor, who sent him for a check-up at the hospital; three weeks later he was dead. My dentist lasted two months after his diagnosis. Now, whenever someone starts telling me about a sudden death, I ask "Pancreatic?" I'm always spot on. The meanest, quickest, deadliest form of cancer. I've also learned that, with luck, you don't suffer pain or thromboses, or struggle to breathe, but just get weaker and weaker. The body simply shuts down, refuses, says goodbye. If you're lucky, you fall asleep and never wake up.

"Would you like something? Can I bring you something?"

"Another pillow."

I brought her the pillow. As I was about to go, she said: "Will you fetch a chair and sit with me?"

"I need to hang up the laundry."

"Will you come back when you've finished?"

What did she want from me? My wife had also wanted me to sit by her bed and hold her hand once, when she had pneumonia. But she hadn't asked me anything, and answered my questions in monosyllables, and I had no idea what I was supposed to do at her bedside. From then on, I brought files along, and worked. Irene had a shelf of books in her room. Maybe I could find one that was interesting?

But when I sat down, she asked: "Will you tell me how it would have been?"

I did not understand.

"How it would have been if I had come to you."

# 3

Sometimes I told my children stories. Usually I got home so late they were already asleep. But when I came home earlier and they were still awake, my wife insisted that I sat down and talked to them. But what were we supposed to discuss, a lawyer entering middle age and a girl and two boys between nine and twelve? Luckily, they enjoyed my stories, the adventures of a boy in the Thirty Years' War, and I enjoyed making them up. By that point my firm had a car and a chauffeur, so on the way home I sat in the back, picking up the threads of my story, working out where I would take it next. But what Irene now wanted – how was I supposed to do that? Talk about her, about me, about us: fiction, but fiction in which we appeared as we really were?

"I don't know . . ."

She said nothing, simply looked at me attentively and expectantly.

"I need a moment."

She nodded, keeping her eyes on me.

I closed my eyes and conjured the old pictures: Irene on the wall, her laugh, her leap, Irene in my arms, Irene at the wheel, Irene telling me I had to get out, kissing me goodbye, dropping me off, driving away. I didn't like the old pictures. I don't know why I did as she asked.

"I went back to my car in the village and drove home. Had you noticed on Saturday that I'd tried to arrange my apartment in a way that would please you? On Sunday I went through the apartment again, taking things away, putting them back, making a bit of a mess here and there so that you wouldn't see straight away how neat and fussy I am; so you would think I was cool and creative. I was afraid that you wouldn't come. I kept looking out the window. I made a pot of tea, forgot to remove the leaves, forgot to take them out of the next pot as well.

"But you came. You came on foot, I saw you coming from a long way off, your upright posture, your light, determined stride – had I ever seen you stroll? You crossed the road, I ran downstairs, opened the door. I wanted to take you in my arms again, but I realized now was not the time, that for you it was not the time.

"As we drank tea you asked if you could stay at my place for a couple of days, as if we were sister and brother. You had your own apartment, but Karl and Peter knew about it, and you didn't want to be there if they came looking for you. Peter would have people looking for you all over town, and you didn't want to be found. You could have gone away, but wanted to go to work again the next day. I asked if they wouldn't find you at work. You said no, not if you told the director that you didn't want to be found. You knew you wouldn't be able to hide for long, but you didn't want to see the pair of them for a couple of days.

"We sat drinking tea on the balcony. There, that morning, I had dreamed of a life together, of this one, and one that was bigger and more beautiful, of a life in a garden with huge trees, of marriage. I would have liked to read some sort of promise into the fact that you wanted to lie low with me, but there was none there. I thought of films in which the hero just takes the woman in his arms, and at first she doesn't want it, and beats his broad chest with her little fists before tenderly snuggling up to him. Had you known that I wouldn't try that? That I wasn't capable of it? That you were safe with me? Did you look down on me for that?

"But then I was overcome by joy that you were staying. At least we'd have a couple days together. Cooking together, eating, talking, reading the newspaper or a book, watching TV, shopping, going for walks. I laughed at you, and you laughed back, relieved that I hadn't been pushy or begged, that there had been no drama. You told me about Karl's rage when he realized the painting was gone, about the row between Karl and Peter, that they didn't pay attention to you and only called after you once you were in the garden. You told it as a funny anecdote, but at the same time you sounded sad – about the both of them, about yourself, maybe about me too, because you'd simply had enough of men. That's how our life in Frankfurt began."

"Where did I sleep?"

"In my bed."

"And you?"

"On the couch."

She nodded. "You went to your firm in the morning, and I went to the museum? And in the evening we cooked together? And on Sunday—"

# 4

"Not so fast. On Tuesday, your apartment was broken into. The apartment manager called you at the museum, and because nothing was missing, everyone assumed that the burglars had been surprised and scared off. You knew they'd been looking for the painting and hadn't found it, and hadn't been after anything else. At dinner you wondered whether they would break into my place, once they found out you were living with me, and you asked if I wanted you to give the painting back."

"No, that's not what I asked."

"It wasn't a serious question. You arched your eyebrow, just as you're doing now. We thought about whether we could prevent a break-in. But if they didn't come the next day, they'd come the day after or the week after. The best thing to do was not to lock the modern safety lock, so they could break in easily, with just a skeleton key.

"That's what we did, not just on Wednesday, but on Thursday and Friday, and because the door didn't need to be broken down, we never found out whether they had searched the apartment. Nothing was missing. You went to the museum early, and stayed late, so that Peter or Karl couldn't intercept you, and I went to my firm, and in the evening we cooked together. On Sunday we had breakfast on the balcony. It was a golden autumn day. We had got through the week unscathed and we started to think that everything might be okay. You wanted to leave soon. But by now I had learned that you loved opera, and I had invited you to *La Bohème*, and you had accepted."

"I didn't nag? I was the sweet little wife in your harmonious little world?"

"I can stop if you want."

She laughed. "No, but we can't just spend our lives on the balcony like an old couple!"

I could have, but not her. "On Monday Karchinger and Kunze sent for me. They were sorry, but we would have to part. The rumour that I'd betrayed a client was just a rumour, and they were confident that, were it to lead to prosecution and a trial, I'd be proven innocent. But that might drag on, and meanwhile, I'd be a liability to the firm, I would need to understand that. An important client already wondered whether we would represent him if I was a partner there. I asked if it was Gundlach, but they told me they couldn't say, and that I should understand that too."

"Betrayal of a client?"

"Working for both parties in a case is legal betrayal. Gundlach had pulled some strings. But not just for me. Your internship at the museum was finished too. The director said he lacked space, and funds, and that he would only keep on the interns he'd eventually hire. And contrary to what he had first believed, and told you, you weren't one of them, to his great regret."

"So on Monday evening we sat on the balcony and . . ."

"No, we didn't sit on the balcony, we went to Sole d'Oro

165

or whatever the best restaurant was back then. We celebrated, because nothing was keeping us in Frankfurt any more – and we could give our furniture to a used furniture store, pack our bags, and head into the world. We were free."

# 5

"I like that."

"And that's exactly what we did. We gave our furniture to a used furniture store and packed our bags. The painting—"

"Was at my mother's."

"The painting was at your mother's, and while I wondered whether we should go to New York or Buenos Aires, whether we should fly or go by sea, you booked flights to New York."

Irene had lain there quietly the entire time, her hands beneath the blanket, her head on the pillows, and her eyes on me. Now she sat up, placed her feet on the ground, and tried to stand up.

"Wait, I'll help you."

"How long have we been sitting here? I have to . . ." She did not say anything else, but looked at me quizzically.

"You don't have to do anything. Did I talk too long? I'll stop and make supper. We forgot to have lunch."

"I have to . . . If only I weren't so tired." She gave me the same questioning look, and once again I didn't understand the question, or know if I should help her up or encourage her to stay in bed. But then her eyes fell shut and she started to fall over, and I caught her and laid her back in bed.

It was late, still light, but the sun had disappeared below the mountains and night would soon fall. I found a tap and a watering can under the balcony and watered Irene's wilted garden; perhaps it would recover by tomorrow and give us a salad. Today there were still plenty of leftovers. In any case, Irene wasn't hungry. Sleepily, without saying a word, she ate a couple bites and let me take her to the toilet then carry her up to bed.

"We have to go see Meredene tomorrow."

"Because of the shopping? I can drive."

"The diapers . . ."

During the day she remained in control of her bodily functions, but she feared what would happen at night. I knew by now where the bed linens and towels were, and I remembered how my wife had changed our babies. I picked out a terry-cloth towel that had worn thin, tore off a strip to make the towel a square, folded the square into a triangle, laid it out underneath her and wrapped it around her.

"It's like riding a bike." She tried to make light of it.

I shrugged. She did not need to know that I hadn't been particularly devoted to looking after my children, not the way modern fathers do. But then I said it anyway. "I was an old-fashioned father. My wife changed all the diapers."

She nodded. "In any case, you watched her do it sometimes. Did you say good night to your children?" She looked at me, ashamed again, almost like she had in the morning. But at the same time she looked secure, as if she felt good in the freshly made bed.

"Good night, Irene." I bent over her and pulled up the blanket. She put her arms around my neck, as she had a couple days before, and once again I was touched by this gesture of trust. I stood up and hurried out, otherwise, I do not know why, the tears would have flowed.

# 6

And so went the days. Irene slept late, then I put her to bed on the balcony. Some days she managed the stairs herself, some days I would carry her. Some days she could even manage the stairs from the balcony to the beach and went to the boulders at the end of the cove, feeling joy at the sand under her bare feet and the water washing around her naked calves.

At first she did not want to, but in the end she let me drive to Meredene alone. Meredene and I drove along a washed-out, overgrown road to the point where it had joined the motorway, drove around the barrier, and after half an hour, reached a town with a supermarket. Our extravagant shopping trip, paid for with my credit card, was perhaps not wholly compatible with the ethos of living in nature; Meredene swore me to secrecy with her people and advised me to not tell Irene. She filled her shopping cart with great enthusiasm and a guilty conscience.

I didn't have a guilty conscience. But I felt forlorn in town, among the shops, adverts, restaurants, cars; and I was annoyed by the bright, cold light in the supermarket, the wide, empty aisles, the sheer range of goods. I calculated: fourteen days ago I had come upon Irene's painting in the

Art Gallery, eight days ago I had arrived at Irene's. It felt like weeks had passed.

Sometimes in the morning I tended Irene's garden, or did the laundry, or tried to fix things: a broken step, a dripping faucet, the Jeep's spare tyre. I took my time and thought about how our story would continue. But sometimes Irene wanted to hear the next installment first thing in the morning, and I had to improvise and slow it down, and elaborate, and embroider. Then we let lunch go by the wayside, and I sat by her bed on the balcony into the late afternoon, telling our story.

I recounted our flight across the Atlantic. As we looked out of the window we saw another plane in the distance, just as, in the middle of the ocean, you can come across another ship – a greeting from the new world you're on your way to. In New York we took a room at the Waldorf Astoria, and enjoyed the city like rich tourists until our money started running out. We went to the Empire State Building, to the Statue of Liberty, to the Metropolitan Museum, to the Guggenheim and the Frick Collection. We walked north through Central Park, past where people had warned us not to go; we ventured into Harlem and to the Bowery, we ate at Café des Artistes and at the Russian Tea Room, and at Tavern on the Green. Irene had never been to New York, and she hadn't seen a film in a long time, and she enjoyed the sights that everyone has images of in their mind, from films or from their brief trips. There were two beds in our room at the Waldorf Astoria, and Irene wanted to know whether either of us had suggested sleeping in the same bed. But she didn't love me, she only liked me, so I found that two beds were more appropriate.

How our days passed – when Irene rested, and we ate, and I talked – depended on how she felt. She did not need the diapers; the mishap she'd had the night Gundlach and Schwind left didn't repeat itself. But she often felt nauseous, and threw up what she had just eaten. Anyway, she had no appetite. She praised my spaghetti carbonara, my mushroom risotto, my goulash, but the only thing she really enjoyed was my salad.

Our days had the kind of ease that, back then, I'd dreamed our life in Frankfurt might.

Once I got carried away and told her so.

"Yes," she said. "But that's a life unto death."

# 7

Day by day it got hotter. The wind from the sea stayed away, and the air that usually feels like a nothing wrapped itself around us, thick and warm. The birds stopped singing and flying, and the plants in the garden withered. Irene banned me from watering them, saying water would soon be in short supply.

"Do you want to move into the house on the beach?"

"Tomorrow, perhaps."

The next day she said it again: "Tomorrow, perhaps," and after that it was as hot in the house on the beach as it was in the house on the hillside. At night, it was even hotter; the stone radiated heat that it had stored during the day. Night brought no relief.

I told her about August in New York, about the wet heat that clung to us like a hot, damp cloth when we stepped out onto the street from an air-conditioned building. Our money ran out and we looked for work. We also moved out of the Waldorf Astoria. The cheap hotel we found was on a street by the Hudson. Two rooms shared a bathroom between them, and if our neighbour forgot to unlock the door to our room when he'd finished, we had to knock on his door, or, if he'd gone out, get the surly porter to come upstairs to unlock it. There was only one bed.

"And?"

"I slept on the floor. It was so hot that I didn't need a blanket. When I could not sleep, I climbed out of the window and sat on the fire escape, looked out on the lit street and the black river. Sometimes you would come and sit with me."

"What did we talk about?"

"You had found a job in Brooklyn as a waitress. I'd found one at McDonald's. We told each other about our jobs. Did you know that McDonald's has its own university? The Hamburger University? When they took me on they promised that once I received my work permit, and if I proved myself, I would be sent to the university. As it was, I was happy when they moved me from the kitchen to the counter."

Irene laughed. "You can't help it, you have to make a career."

"But not at McDonald's. I wanted to be a lawyer again and I had found out that while I couldn't take the bar exam in New York without first getting a law degree, I could in California. So I wanted to go to California. At the same time, we liked New York; we had seen how much the city had to offer, even to people with no money. We made friends, we had an apartment lined up. But then . . ."

I wasn't sure if I should tell her what had just popped into my head. Well, it hadn't occurred to me just like that; during my first trip to New York, when I was still a student and couldn't afford a hotel, and stayed with friends of friends in Brooklyn, I'd wandered into a café to get coffee, and this was the café in which I now imagined Irene waitressing. The restaurant had the standard menu and the standard football above the bar; the staff were friendly in the standard rough-and-ready way, and the atmosphere was completely unerotic. It was a restaurant like any other, except for one thing.

"Then?"

"Then I came to visit you at work, and saw that you had to waitress topless, and I took you away, and we bought a used car, and left the next day."

"You can't just . . . It was my job, right? If it didn't bother me . . . Were you jealous?"

"Think what you like. I am telling the story. I have to look away in our bedroom, while you show the entire world?"

"Understood." Irene smiled – teasing, friendly, pityingly? What right did she have to smile at me with pity? But it was my own fault. I'd sensed that the story was taking a delicate turn, and I should have just dropped it. I didn't want to be jealous. I wanted to come off well. I would have liked to rescue Irene from a rapist in Central Park, to snatch her back on a crosswalk from a drunk-driver, to foil a pickpocket on 5th Avenue. I would have liked to be a hero. But I couldn't think of any deed that didn't sound corny, that didn't sound like I was trying to build myself up.

"Do you like cars? Ours was old, a 1956 Chevrolet Bel Air, green with a white roof, white fins and whitewall tyres. Its hood ornament was a cross between an airplane and a rocket – it flew ahead, and all we had to do was follow."

# 8

When I carried Irene to bed that evening, she shifted to one side and pointed to the other. She wanted me to sit down.

"Do you remember why Parsifal never asked?"

"Didn't his mother teach him never to ask unnecessary questions? And he took it more literally than she had meant?"

"Why don't you ask anything?"

"On the first evening you evaded my questions, and I thought . . ."

"That first evening is a while ago."

I shrugged. "My grandparents asked only the most basic questions. Do you want to learn to play piano? To play tennis? To dance? And I too asked only for what I needed. I'd like to go to the theatre, to the opera, or on holiday to Spain with friends – could you give me the money? Until one day they raised my allowance and I didn't have to ask for money any more. They were truly generous."

"What was it like in your family? With your wife and your children? Did you ask them a lot of questions?"

Under Irene's questions, I began to feel uncomfortable. "I thought I was supposed to ask more questions. But instead you are interrogating me."

"Sorry." She placed her hand on mine. "Sleep well."

I went down to the house on the beach and sat on the bench on the veranda. The water was so smooth that it reflected the sickle of the moon like a mirror, and made no sound on the pebbles. I missed that sound, and I would have preferred to see the moon dancing on the waves. I was upset. Did Irene want to psychoanalyse me? Therapize me? What business of hers was it how many questions I asked my wife and children? Some families ask more questions than others. With our children, my wife handled the questions and the talking. And with her – the beauty of it was that we understood each other without questions. She lived her life and I mine, and I was there for her when she needed me. Did I need to justify that to Irene?

Parsifal. I remembered that on his first visit to the castle he didn't ask the old man about his suffering, and didn't relieve him of that suffering, so lived under a kind of curse until, on his second visit, he asked the redeeming question. But how did he know that he was supposed to ask the question that time? How was I supposed to know what sort of questions Irene wanted me to ask? Unlike Parfisal, I had at least asked about her illness.

# 9

The next day we drove west. Sometimes the highway led us over long bridges, or in loops above and below other highways, through the backyards of cities; and we saw only crumbling roads, deserted parking lots, boarded-up houses, trash, and beyond, the silhouette of skyscrapers. Sometimes it would leave us in the middle of a city, at a crossing with traffic lights, honking cars, rushing pedestrians, offices and shops. Over farmlands it spun out like a broad ribbon, flat, or gently rising and falling, far from the towns and villages named on the road signs, far from farmhouses and factories too. We saw forests, cornfields, pastures, a couple of cattle on the pastures here and there, behind the cornfields maybe a silo, or a smoking chimney, or a steaming tower. On the third day all we saw were wheat fields. Under the huge sky, they stretched to the horizon; your eye lost itself in the distance. The music on the radio changed, we heard banjo and fiddle, accordion and harmonica, catchy songs about women and love, simple ballads about struggle and death. The news reported on rodeos, quarrels and fistfights, births, deaths, school and church fairs, run-over dogs, runaway cats, false alarms, and that Jesus loves us. The highway had narrowed into a two-lane road, and the heat shimmered on the asphalt.

We drove slowly, and Irene put her seat back, rolled the window down and stretched out her legs out. After the first verse she knew the melody of a song and would hum along with the rest. From time to time, something on the news would trigger her imagination and she would spin it into a story. How John Dempsey caught the biggest fish of the summer. What the patrons at Crossroads Café had started fighting over. Why Catalina Fisk didn't call the ambulance, although she could have been saved.

"Are you afraid of death?"

Irene thought about it so long, eyes closed, that I wondered if she had forgotten my question or even fallen asleep. It happened more and more that in the middle of a conversation she lost herself to other thoughts, or to the fatigue that was her constant companion. "The things I missed out on . . . Is that fear of death, that things will forever be unsaid, undone, unlived? But really, they already are now, and have been for a while. The time to put things right has long since passed."

Should I keep asking questions? Had Parsifal asked the old man more questions after the first? Where does compassion end and intrusion begin? "What would you like to put right? What you did with dyed hair and sunglasses?"

She opened her eyes and looked at me. "Oh, that . . . No, I would like to see my daughter again or just to know how she is, what she's doing with her life." She saw the question in my eyes. "I got married in East Germany and – it was a surprise, I was already too old – I had a daughter. I didn't want to take her away from my husband. It must have been hard enough for him that I vanished without a trace, but to take Julia as well . . . in his pedantic way, he really loved us both."

What made you choose someone like that? I wanted to ask. I'd also have liked to know why she left her husband and daughter, and never got back in touch with them, and what she had to fear, after the time of dyed hair and sunglasses. Had she actually killed someone? What had she said to Gundlach? That she had been involved. That could mean anything. "I can take the boat to Rock Harbour and call my firm and have them find out about Julia."

"Can you do it after I'm gone? And see if she needs anything? And make sure she gets what's left of my mother's estate?" She took my hand.

I didn't feel good. What if Julia really needed something? An education? Medical treatment that her insurance wouldn't pay for? Psychotherapy? Rehab? What if she wasn't just a drug addict, but dealt drugs as well or walked the streets to pay for the drugs, or committed petty crimes – or even serious ones? Money for a defence lawyer or treatments or a course of study was one thing. But what if I had to go look for her in the red-light district in Berlin, night after night, and finally discovered a stupid, common person, would it be my job to help her get her act together? I had refused, even with good friends, to be a godfather to children, because the responsibility was too much for me. But I nodded.

"Yes?"

"Yes."

"She was a sweet girl. I left when she was coming into the terrible twos, but she didn't really throw tantrums, she would sulk and pout with tears in her eyes, and when I explained to her why she couldn't have what she wanted, she stopped straight away."

Irene cried. At first I heard quiet whimpering, then loud

howling, and then I could scarcely recognize her face, the crumpled forehead, the mouth torn open; she threw her head from side to side, then buried her face in the pillow.

Crying: that cheap trick women use to put us in the wrong. I cannot stand it, and I thought highly of my wife for the fact that she stopped crying soon after we were married, because she understood that the crying game wasn't fair, that it repulsed me, that I refused to play it. I can say with pride that my children didn't cry either; when my eldest was eight, he broke his arm and ran home from the playground, and rode with my wife and I to the hospital, without shedding a tear.

But how was I supposed to explain to Irene that her pain wasn't my responsibility; that I was an inappropriate recipient of her tears? She kept crying and held onto my hand so that I couldn't just get up and go. Finally, I couldn't stand her crying, her face buried in the pillow, her shaking shoulders, or the way I was sitting awkwardly beside her, and I took her in my arms and rocked her, and made soothing sounds until she fell asleep.

When she woke up in my arms, she looked at me kindly, even happily, and smiled and said: "Thank you." I didn't understand what she was thanking me for, but I didn't want to question something that seemed to please her, so I smiled back.

# 10

Then the harvest began in the fields of the Midwest. Irene had once seen pictures of combine harvesters, rolling in unison over wheat fields, and asked: "Where are the combine harvesters?" In her memory, flags flew from the machines, and the operators, male and female, laughed with joy – more Soviet propaganda than American reality, but a couple of flags on the combine couldn't hurt, and we couldn't see the faces of the drivers. So on we drove. For hours on end combines would pop into view, sometimes in a row, though more often just one monster machine. They all flew flags.

We slept in motels. The rooms were always big, with two beds, and a TV screwed to the wall near the ceiling. There was a soda machine with Coke and Sprite and ice cubes in the lobby, and before we went to sleep we would lie in bed watching TV, drinking the beer and eating the chips we'd bought in the last town.

"I was worried about what awaited us in San Francisco and how we would get by there. I wanted to talk about it, but you didn't want to plan, you wanted to take things as they came. I think you thought I was petty. Actually, why did you choose a pedantic husband?"

She looked at me that way again.

"Not that you should think I'm jealous. I'm simply interested why you did what you did. Too many questions already? You just said I should ask more questions."

"No, it's not too many. Helmut was like East Germany. I liked that he was reliable and caring, if maybe a little paternalistic. The way I felt about you – I can't recall. Are you petty?"

What a question! I take things seriously, sometimes too seriously, I aim for precision in everything I do, sometimes too much precision: again and again I have difficulty understanding why people become emotional in difficult situations instead of solving the problem rationally; and I find it's often the little things that people stumble over, that cause them to fail. But I don't split hairs, or bear grudges, and I'm not cheap. Petty?

I left the question unanswered and drove with Irene over the Rocky Mountains. We saw a lot of forest, calm and wild rivers, water that fell from high cliffs – from afar, a silver beam, up close a tumbling, spraying roar – the snow on the peaks, the quick-changing weather, the terrible thunderstorms echoing off the mountains like the noise of a battle. I would have liked to rescue Irene from a bear, but we never met one, nor would I have known how if we had. Instead, a lost or abandoned dog joined us at a rest spot, a black thing, with white, spotted nose, chest and paws, anxious and trustingly demanding at the same time. It accompanied us everywhere, jumping and circling us. When we drove with the windows open, and Irene stretched her feet out the front window, it stuck its head out the rear one and couldn't get enough of the smells of the world.

"What was its name?"

"I don't know. You tell me."

"Was it a he or a she?"

"A she."

Irene fell asleep before she could tell me its name. Night was falling, but the heat didn't lift – the dry, red-hot, parching heat that we had woken up to and fallen asleep with for days. I made gazpacho from canned tomatoes and Irene ate a few spoonfuls before she fell asleep again. I let her sleep on the balcony, and brought a mattress out for myself as well. It was no cooler than inside the house, but there was more air.

I woke up in the middle of the night and remembered. I had described the dog that the children had brought home one day. They had found it at the park where they met their friends in the afternoon; it was ownerless – didn't have a dog tag anyway – and they had taken it into their hearts. It was really social; my wife liked when she sat on the sofa and it lay down next to her with its head on her leg, and she called it her warm little bundle. I made sure that we did not keep it. I was bothered by the dirt it brought into the house, the mess when the children played with it, and the damage to our Biedermeier sofa, which, when my wife wasn't there, it would sometimes bite and lick; and the thought of having to take it for walks when the children grew tired of it. No one complained when it was gone.

I have always seen myself as a generous husband and father. My wife got all the help she wanted in the house, and her own car as well, and whatever the children needed, they got – even when they only thought they needed something, but it turned out they did not. Had I, in small things, been a little petty sometimes? How did I know that my children would grow tired of the dog? How did I know that losing

184

him didn't upset my wife and children? Did I hear no complaint from them only because we talked so little? What else was left unsaid?

My wife's accident came to mind. I lay on my back, arms crossed behind my head, and looked at the sky. I knew the Southern Cross from the Australian and New Zealand flags; I looked for it, but could not find it. The Milky Way got me thinking of my mother, of whom I have almost no memory; I do know that my birth was by caesarean and that she didn't breastfeed me, because at the time doctors advised against it after a caesarean. A tiny, bright dot arced through the sky; I followed it with my eyes and fell asleep.

# 11

Irene enjoyed the drive from the Rocky Mountains to the Pacific. The clear light, the dry grass – brown, but lit gold in morning and evening; the orchards, row after row of trees planted with such precision that their shadows whisked over our car like the beat of a metronome; the vineyards growing not on hillsides but in valleys; the place names that bore witness to the Spaniards or Russians who once had settled there. Irene imagined the people from the Crimea who had found their way to California and founded Sebastopol, the stoves glowing between the vines on cold nights, the rush of pink when the orchards bloomed in spring. Before we reached the Pacific, we crossed one last mountain range. From its heights we could see the fog that hung in the valleys and over the ocean, a fog so thick that it seemed no sun could dissolve it. It was late morning, and we sat on the brown grass, the dog at our feet, and drank the red wine we had bought at a winery. We felt sleepy, dozed off, and woke up. The fog was gone and the Pacific shimmered in the midday sun.

"I lay still. While we were asleep, you had turned towards me and laid your arm over my chest."

Irene smiled. "You're becoming daring."

"You laid your arm across my chest, not the other way round."

She laughed. "I see. And then what?"

"You woke up, left your arm on my chest for a moment longer, then sat up and looked out at the Pacific. I sat up too, and you leant your shoulder against mine."

"How did you feel with my arm on your chest and my shoulder on yours?"

Why do women always need to hear how you feel? They have to hear it – knowing it isn't enough. It's like in the army, where it's not enough that you serve loyally, you have to face the flag every morning and pledge allegiance. It's a ritual of submission, one which I refused to surrender to with my wife, and one which she eventually abandoned. At some point, she gave up asking me how I felt.

"Good," I said, and we drove down to the ocean, and along the coast towards San Francisco. Irene had seen *The Birds*, and in Bodega, I showed her the schoolhouse from the film. Then we went down to the water, and walked the beach, and I told her about the waves that suddenly, out of calm water, can rear up and snatch anyone walking too close and not give them back.

Suddenly, I was afraid for her. She had no choice. She was walking on the edge, and at some point the cancer would take hold of her and not let go.

As we drove over the Golden Gate Bridge, the sun set. It dipped into the fog, and from one moment to the next the Pacific was gray, hostile, merciless. But the city was still awash in light. I would have liked to hear the song on the radio that I had once heard and liked. Something about San Francisco, or California, or both, but the title escaped me, and all I could remember was a bit of melody. I sang it to Irene, and she recognized the song, but she couldn't remember the title either. Whatever – we had arrived.

"Here we are." I smiled at Irene.

"Yes," she smiled back. "Here we are."

# 12

I hardly ever got sick. When I was, I did as my grandparents taught me: be as little of a bother as possible, need as little as possible, ask as little as possible. It's bad enough that when you're ill, you don't function; you shouldn't get in the way of others functioning more than you have to. And that is how my wife and I handled illness in our family. In the war, the sick had to fight in soaking trenches, or flee for their lives through snow and ice, or wait for bombs to drop on their freezing cellars. Do we not have reason to feel satisfied and grateful that, unlike them, we can lie in bed when we're sick?

In the beginning, Irene was similar. She only asked for something when she was truly helpless, and then she was visibly embarrassed, and apologized and thanked me. With each day, my help became more of a given, and Irene had more needs and requests. Instead of three large meals, many small ones; instead of the alternatives of a bed in the bedroom and a bed on the balcony, a bed on this and on that side of the balcony as well, and on the veranda of the house, on the beach, and underneath the acacia by the steps. Instead of a request for a glass of water, "I'm thirsty", and instead of "Thank you", a smile, or nothing. When she felt nauseous, and vomiting brought no relief, and she had to continue gagging and spitting, and the bucket was too far away, or there was no tissue ready, or if I didn't hold her right, she snapped at me.

I found that hard to put up with. I could not imagine that she would have wanted to be treated like that. So how was it okay to treat me that way? Does cancer or the proximity of death grant special privilege? I couldn't see it, and I remain determined not to claim special privilege in the same situation. But maybe I couldn't, as I had been doing, brush off her embarrassed apologies and thanks, and say it was nothing, without accepting that I'd be taken at my word. Maybe it was good that she took my help for granted now. Maybe fairness isn't everything.

The evening after our arrival in San Francisco, she was again different. She said please when she needed something and thanked me when she got it, and apologized for all the trouble she was causing. It was as if she wanted to put some distance between us, and turn me into someone she wasn't already tied to, from whom she could withdraw. She reminded me of my little daughter, who in summer camp learned that she could get along without us, and let us know, when she got back, that she was independent, and that we could no longer take her for granted. Irene was turning away.

"I can manage," she said as she got up after dinner and went to the stairs.

"Where do you want to sleep?"

"On the balcony."

She walked up the stairs, slowly, laboring, bowed, walking her hands on the steps. I stood nearby, ready to help her, but she didn't need me.

I washed the dishes, cleaned up the kitchen and set the table for morning. Then I poured myself what was left of the wine and took the glass out onto the balcony. I heard Irene walk from the bedroom to the bathroom, shower, and return to the bedroom. It was hot, like the entire day had been and the night before and the day before that, and I noticed that I had come to like the night heat; it wasn't less, but it had lost its bite.

Then I heard Irene call and went into the kitchen.

# 13

She came down the stairs. Her right hand grazed the wall, to support her if needed, but she held herself upright and placed one foot surely in front of the other. She held her head at a slight angle, and looked at me. She was naked.

What went through my head as she came down the stairs! That she must have taken the last of her cocaine. How pale, how deathly pale her body looked aside her sun-tanned face, neck and arms. How weary it was, with its tired breasts, the tired skin around her belly, and yet how beautiful. That weary beauty was still beauty. What the kids in the Art Gallery had thought about her hips, thighs and feet, and how wrong it was. What I had projected onto her: softness and seduction, resistance and refusal, and that in the end she was just a woman with a life of her own. How courageously she had lived it; how timidly I had lived mine. That she had shown the children she'd taken in more love than I had shown mine. That her body's weariness moved me. How close that feeling was to desire.

She spoke with her eyes. She was playing a role for me, but not performing. She wasn't the young Irene, we both knew, but was old – as I was old. That at this point, she had little left to offer but love. That she was inviting me to also offer just that, and to acknowledge that that was what I wanted. But that she also enjoyed the game, the self-reference, and my admiring gaze.

Then she came down and gave her entire body to our embrace, chest to chest, belly to belly, thighs to thighs. My hands felt her skin; she was like silk paper, soft, dry, fragile. I knew that I would soon carry her to her room. But there was no hurry.

# 14

The next day, I made a double bed in her room from two singles, and pushed our mattresses together on the balcony. I was hesitant to share a bed with Irene on the balcony, where Kari might appear at any moment. But she shook her head. "He only comes when he thinks I might be in danger. If a helicopter appears, or a boat, any strangers."

Never again was Irene so lively as the evening when she took her last cocaine. We never made love again either; she was too weak, and she was happy when we held each other. Something else changed. She kept wanting me to tell her stories, but after our night together, she wanted to hear something different. "Would you tell me how it might have gone if we had met as students?"

"How could we have met as students? You were political, you had admirers, you were invited to parties and openings, you got married early – all I did was go to lectures and seminars and sit in the library."

"But now you know you could have met me . . . Didn't you ever go to the Cave?"

"No."

"But you knew about it? And where it was?"

So when the library closed at ten, I didn't go home, but

to the Cave. It was an underground club on two levels, with a bar and tables above, and a stage and dance floor below; the air was full of smoke, and a couple of kids were playing jazz. The music had no melody – was that free jazz? Was The Black – black skirts, black jeans, black sweaters, black jackets – existentialism? Was that what lent cool ease to the way people moved, sat down, stood up, lit each other's cigarettes and smoked, and raised their glasses and drank? What let the men, who in fact wanted to get near the beautiful women, look so blasé, and the women look at the men as if they were tedious? I looked around and—

Irene laughed loudly. "Where did you get that *nouvelle vague* cliché? By the end of the sixties, nobody was wearing black; the girls at university wanted all the excitement they'd missed in their little towns, and the boys tried to impress us with grand speeches about critical theory and revolutionary praxis. Did all that really pass you by?"

"Like I told you, I did nothing but study."

"And later you did nothing but work? The firm took you on, and you took over, and made it bigger and bigger?"

"What do you want from me?"

"I don't want anything from you." She took me in her arms. "I'm trying to picture your life. Your walled-in life. Maybe if you live behind walls, the world outside is bound to become a cliché."

I didn't know what to say. My work often took me abroad and I kept an open mind wherever I went. At home, I read two newspapers, the business and finance sections first, but also politics and culture. I was better informed about the world than most. Just because I wasn't familiar with the student fashions of the late sixties – did that make me someone who lived behind walls?

She felt me holding back in her embrace, and pulled me closer. "Did you never go visit your kids at university? And go to their hangouts, their parties?"

"My children went to boarding school when they were fourteen, and they stayed in England. I went to Cambridge for their graduations, terrific occasions, all pomp and circumstance. And I was there when my youngest won the Boat Race against Oxford."

"Do you see each other often?"

"They all stayed in England, the eldest and the middle one as lawyers, the youngest with his own software company. I go over whenever a grandchild is born or the three of them celebrate something. I don't want to be a burden."

Slowly and gently, Irene ran her hand down my back. "My pure fool. You always want to do the right thing." She said it again, tenderly, and sadly. "My pure fool."

Again, I had no idea what she meant. I started crying, not knowing why, and not why now. I was ashamed, I felt ridiculous, but I couldn't stop myself. I missed my children, not the children who now lived in England, but the teenagers they once were, and all I had missed: their adolescence, their school conflicts, the hobbies and friendships and first loves, the questions about what to study. When, back then, I picked up my children at the airport, they weren't returning home, but were only visiting on holiday, and often they immediately left for a language course or tennis camp. Back then, my children never complained, but still, now, I felt sorry for them. I felt sorry for myself as well, and I was crying for myself as much as I was crying for them, and for my wife, who had always been opposed to England. Had I really thought that was what was best for them? Or had I just given myself an easy and comfortable child-free life?

"Go on, cry," Irene kept stroking my back. "Everything will be all right."

But how? Anyway, I took in her comforting attention, and it wove together with my self-reproach and self-pity into a blanket, under which I cried myself to sleep.

# 15

"I think this is the last time," Irene said the next morning. "I want to go down the stairs to the beach once more."

As we went down, she with one hand on the rail and the other on my shoulder, I too knew this was the last time. She stopped on each step and gathered her strength for the next, then put down the right, always first the right foot, and then the left. Then she rested until she had again gathered her strength. She breathed heavily, and couldn't speak, and every now and then she gave me an exhausted or apologetic or ironic smile.

I could have cried again. What was wrong with me, last night and today? When Irene and I found each other, it was clear that we would have each other only briefly. But that was a truth somewhere out there, not between us, where so much happened, where there was so much life, so much promise. Now, on the long way down the stairs, the shortness of our time became a truth between us, and I could not bear it. I don't need anyone, I had always thought – perhaps to be happy, but not to survive, and I had survived on my own. Now, I didn't know how I could survive without Irene, how I would approach my children differently without her, or do my work differently, or make my life different. How I would fall asleep, or wake up without her.

But I did not cry. I tried to go down the stairs slowly, one foot in front of the other, step by step, as if it were the most normal thing in the world. Then she stopped on one step for a long time, until she caught her breath. "You said that English legal firms are taking over German ones. Why don't you open a branch of your firm in England with the two older ones?" I thought of the distance my children maintained with me. "They did follow in your footsteps after all."

A couple of steps further down, she stopped again. "My daughter – you'll have to see whether you think you can tell her about me. I don't want you to upset her. I want you to do her good. If you do her good by doing nothing, then do nothing."

Then we had reached the end of the stairs. "How lovely," she said, standing in the water. Everything was lovely, the warm water, the smooth sea, the pebbles and fish and plants at the bottom, the sky, still morning-blue, without the haze of the day's heat. Irene leant into my embrace, took everything in, and rested. "Can we make it to the boulder at the end of the cove?"

But after only a few steps she felt sick, and she threw up what she had just eaten. We took a break and sat down on the veranda of the house on the beach. "And if we had met as children?"

"I remember the schoolhouse, yellow brick with red sandstone ornaments, and its two equal halves, one for girls and one for boys. Like the building, the schoolyard was divided into two equal halves, and during the main break the girls and boys from grades one to four would walk, two by two, in two big circles overseen by some of the older children, who were themselves overseen over by a teacher. The older children who didn't have to oversee us were free to move around, and bothered us, and hit us, and took our apples and pretzels – it was a game for them, it wasn't about the apples or pretzels, but about getting away with it.

"I was an anxious child. I was afraid of school, of the teachers, of the big kids, of the walk to school, where the big kids bothered me, and sometimes hit me or took something from me. Of arriving late, and again and again I was late; though I left on time; I would dawdle out the way, dreading school. For a long time, I saw my life at school through a fog, without understanding what it was about, or what mattered.

"Then one day, I realized that the girl with blonde pigtails in the other circle was the girl I sometimes saw in the store where my grandmother sent me to shop. Like me, she brought a metal pail that the grocer would fill with either whole or skimmed milk. And like me she had a note telling the grocer what to pack in her bag. Unlike me, she didn't give him her purse, but paid like a grown-up; slowly, the tip of her tongue between her lips, she took out notes and coins, until she had the closest possible amount, and counted her change just as carefully. We didn't talk to each other. I wasn't brave enough, and especially not as long as I still paid like a child.

"So mathematics became the first subject in which I made an effort. I can still remember the first time that I took out the notes and coins from my purse and counted the change. The girl wasn't there; it took several weeks before we ran into each other at the shop and she saw that I could do what she could. She gave me a quick look – 'About time' – and did not put the tip of her tongue between her lips when she counted, perhaps because I did not do it. I didn't give the grocer the shopping list any more, but read out what I was supposed to buy, and she did the same. I knew by now where she lived; without either of us making a detour, but just taking a different route, we could walk most of the way home together. But neither of us proposed it.

"Sometimes I would follow her home from school at a distance. I don't think she ever noticed. But then something happened to her that I knew all too well. Two big boys came up behind her, then they were next to her, and then they were pushing her against a fence. She fought back, but didn't shout. I heard the boys laughing, yelling 'Come on' and 'Give it up'. I ran, ran into the first boy with all my strength and hit the other in the stomach as hard as I could. I took the girl's hand and I ran off with her, round the next corner, and into a garden and behind a bush. But the boys didn't follow us.

"After a while I walked her home. I didn't let go of her hand, and didn't try to pull it from mine. In front of her house I asked what her—"

"Is that a true story?"

"She was not blonde, she was dark, and she was not called Irene, which is what I was about to call her, but Barbara. For two or three weeks we walked home together hand in hand, then she was gone, and I had forgotten all about her until you asked me about school. If it had been you, and you hadn't moved away, but had stayed . . ." I took Irene's hand.

"Yes."

# 16

We made it to the boulder at the end of the cove. Then she couldn't go on. I carried her back to the stairs, and up them, and laid her on the bed on the balcony. It was so early that the sun was still shining on the bed; I opened the sun umbrella and positioned it.

"Do you smell something?"

"No. What do you smell?"

"Fire. But maybe I'm imagining it."

I went through the house and checked the gas oven and the boiler and the candles that in the past few days we had sometimes lit. I checked our provisions; in two or three days I would have to drive into town. I would have liked to have had some morphine on hand in case Irene was in real pain. Maybe Kari could get hold of some – or some heroin?

When I got back to the balcony, Irene was asleep. I sat next to her, and watched her. The hair, combed away from her face and bunched at the nape of her neck. Her forehead lined with wrinkles, and the deep grooves in her cheeks. The mouth with lips grown thin, the round, prominent chin, the empty skin beneath it at her throat. She looked severe. I made all sorts of faces, but couldn't find one that would have etched the grooves in her cheeks, nor carved the crow's feet at the corners of her eyes – laughing joy at the world, or a fearful rejection of it, with squinting eyes? It wasn't a sweet face. And yet it was precious to me. It held the joys, and fears, and ruptures in her life.

The longer I looked at it, the more I thought I understood her face. There was both joy and fear around the eyes; harshness and softness in the cheeks; and the thin lips were ready to break into an enchanting smile.

She opened her eyes. "What are you looking at?"

"I'm just looking at you."

She didn't like the answer and shook her head, smiling.

"When I look at your face, I see what I know about you, and what I still don't know. I'm putting it together. Each time I look at you, I know you better. Each time, I love you more."

"I dreamt I was riding on a train, first on an express train, and then on a commuter train, and as I got off, I already knew it was the wrong station, but I got off anyway and it was the wrong station, so desolate and run-down, as if no train had stopped there in years. I went through the station building to the square outside, and everything was deserted there too: no taxis, no buses, no people. But then I saw Karl and Peter, both sitting on their suitcases, old-fashioned things without wheels or pull-out handles, as if they were waiting to be picked up. When I went up to them, they didn't look up or move, and it seemed to me that they had died long ago, and were sitting there, dead, on their suitcases. I felt a shock – but not like something hitting me, more like something cold, slowly creeping up my spine. Then I woke up."

"I can't interpret dreams. Dreams are just dreams, as my

wife used to say. But when the three of you talked about the end of the world and of art and of alternatives – weren't you at the station where the last train had left long ago? Weren't you sitting dead on your suitcases?" I had wanted, but forgotten, to ask her just after the others had left: "Do you really believe what you said?"

She looked around. I brought her pillows so that she could sit up. She arranged herself, and gave me the look I had come to know, and which bespoke tenderness, but also sadness that I didn't understand what she wanted me to. "My pure fool," she said. "You go through life fighting your battles like knights fought their tournaments, and like them, you don't see that it's the end of an era – that it's just a game of mirrors now. I love how keen you are to trudge from task to task, dutifully doing yet another merger, yet another acquisition, as if it meant something. It moves me, and it makes me sad."

I wanted to protest. I wanted to justify what I did, to explain that mergers and acquisitions mean something. That the battles I fought were more than a game of mirrors. That nothing had come to an end; that everything went on and on.

"Don't worry. When people talk about the world, they're usually talking about themselves. Perhaps it's just that I can't bear that I'm coming to an end, without the world ending too. Come here!"

We held one another, both lost in our thoughts, but still together. Then my thoughts grew stale, and I was sad, because I too sensed the barrier that kept us from fully understanding and feeling for each other. Not just Irene and me – from early on, a pane of glass had prevented me from really reaching others – my wife, my children, my friends. I was, always, on my own.

Again I could have – but I had already cried enough the evening before. In any case, I tried to remain present in our embrace and to release all the other feelings, all the other thoughts as soon as they came. I didn't find it easy.

# 17

The next morning, Irene smelled fire again.

"Wouldn't Kari be here if something was wrong? Should I go see Meredene? We need to stock up anyway."

She shook her head. "Don't go. You're right — if something's wrong, Kari will come." She looked at me anxiously. "I'm not sure I'm going to be able to hold it in today. I feel so weak — I've never been this weak before. I was sick once, when I still had the kids. My temperature kept rising, and finally I went to bed and I was grateful that I didn't have to do anything, and could just lie there. Actually it can be nice, just lying there. Lying down, sleeping, maybe even dying. Would you tell me something?"

"Well . . . I have two memories of my mother. Right after the war, my parents and I moved from north to south Germany, and we made the trip in the trailer of the moving van, which had a cab with a bench seat and a window, like in a truck, but without the steering wheel or engine. Sitting on my mother's lap and looking out the window — that is one memory. The other is being with my mother at a playground once. It was behind the empty lot where the synagogue had stood until 1938, a small, oblong park with trees and benches and a sand box.

"I remember that it was evening, and it was getting dark. My mother was sitting with me in the sandpit, building a sandcastle. She had brought a flat piece of wood with her and she used it as a roof on the first level of the tower to build a second storey on. She had brought a little pail of water with her, that helped, but still, the tower was a miracle: on the second floor one could see into the room through the door and out through the window on the other side. She worked with utter concentration, and was lost in the project as though I wasn't there. Still, I was totally happy. She was with me and only with me; she was doing something for me and me alone. By the time it got dark, she was done. The street lights came on, gas lanterns giving off a soft light, and we sat and looked at the castle. I'm sure it had a rampart and one or two other buildings, but the thing I remember most clearly is the tower with two storeys, and I saw Rapunzel roll down her hair and the prince climb up to her. Then I looked up, and a little blonde girl was standing next to me. She was looking at the castle too, with bright blue-gray eyes and with an awestruck, slightly crooked smile."

"You just made that up." Irene reproached me gently.

"Yes. The strange thing is, now I wonder if I made up the whole story. There really was a playground, but why do I have no other memories of playing with my mother, at home or outside, and why would she have done it that particular evening? She was not especially good with her hands, she was impatient, far too impatient to build a two-storey tower out of sand. Sometimes she would read me fairy tales. Did I imagine a fairy tale of my own? But that evening is in my memory, not as fantasy but reality, and I can see it all before me, clear as day: the sandpit, my mother in a blue

208

dress, the castle in the twilight, then in the dark, then in the light of the gas lanterns."

"How old were you when your mother died?"

"Four. It couldn't have been long after that."

"How did she die?"

"She drove into a tree."

Irene looked at me as if she was waiting for me to say more.

"She was a good driver. Sometimes she would take me with her, I would sit or stand next to her on the passenger seat. There were no seatbelts or booster seats back then, and I loved it when she drove fast. I felt completely safe."

Irene was still waiting.

"My grandparents said once that she was drunk. That she was an alcoholic. But my grandparents were against the marriage, they didn't like my mother and never had a good word to say about her. I would have smelt it if she'd been an alcoholic. Children smell those things."

Irene took my hand. I could tell exactly what she was thinking. Like your wife, she thought. I didn't like that thought, but her eyes grew heavy, and I thought it was better that she slept the thought away than if I contradicted it. She fell asleep, and I held her hand and resented her.

# 18

Then I too smelled smoke. It had the sharp, sweet scent of eucalyptus; it was faint yet penetrating and almost intoxicating. I stood up and looked around, but I saw no smoke and no fire. The mountains, the cove, the trees, the bush, the jetty, the sea – everything looked the same.

Suddenly, Kari was standing next to me and signalled that I should come along. I wrote a note for Irene saying Kari had come and wanted to show me something. I thought we would take the Jeep, but Kari headed up the mountain in quick, light strides, and I struggled to keep up with him. I only knew the way the Jeep took, through the mountains along the coast into the rolling plain where the two farms lay. Now Kari led me up a path on one of the mountains. We went ever higher, the cove was small and blue beneath us like an illustration from *Treasure Island*. After half an hour we stood on the mountaintop.

The view stretched all the way to the mountain range on the far side of the plain. Even before I saw the fire, patches and lines of reddish gold on the mountains, I saw the smoke billowing black into the clear sky. When it drifted over a gorge where the fire was burning, it lit up gold-red. It lit up, too, when it passed over a mountain whose far side was already ablaze; the ember glow announced that the flames would soon reach the summit and crown it with fire. Then they ate their way down the mountain, and by the time they reached the bottom, they had devoured everything above, and left only embers, black ash, and charred wood.

Fire engines with flashing lights sped down the stretches of motorway that were visible. Helicopters flew over them.

"Will the fire reach us?"

"The plain is wide. But it's dry, and if the fire jumps the motorway . . ." Kari shrugged.

"Then?"

"I don't know. It depends on the wind. We still can't smell much and we still can't see too much smoke – the wind is still weak. But if it picks up . . ."

"Have you had a wildfire here before?"

"No, not here. Further north, though. The fire makes the wind and the wind drives the fire."

"Oh God!" I saw a town burning at the foot of the mountains, the one where Meredene and I had gone shopping.

Kari stayed on the hilltop. I went down to Irene. She was up. "I know. The mountains are on fire. What will Meredene and her family and the old couple do?"

"They can come here. The motorway's still open, someone will pick them up."

"And the animals?"

I imagined one of the children driving the animals to us in the cove, and if the fire reached us, into the water. I could already hear the cows lowing and the pigs squealing and the chickens clucking. But nobody came, not the people from the farms and not the animals. I don't know what became of them.

I was not worried about us. The boat was moored to the jetty, I filled the tank, and tried the engine, and it ran smoothly and reliably. I took a mattress out to the boat and made a bed in front of the helm and loaded food, lots of water, blankets. I stored all the towels and linen I could find in the house on the beach so that if the fire came I could soak them and protect the wooden roof structure, and windows. I brought everything we would need down to the old house as well. If the fire came we would go out onto the sea and wait until it was over. And then, presumably, if not into the upper house, we would at least be able to move back into the house on the beach.

In late afternoon, smoke drifted over the cove. Ash rained down, very light, very fine; it landed on our skin, and in the folds in our clothes, and on our teeth, leaving a bitter taste behind. I found my way up the mountain and squatted down next to Kari. Beneath a murky, yellow-gray sky the edge of the plain was in flames; the fire had managed to leap the motorway. The forest was burning gold-red, and sometimes, as if an invisible hand were reaching into the fire and hurling a flame, a tree or bush far beyond the fire line would burst into flames, followed by the surrounding grass.

"When will the fire get here?"

As if in answer to my question, the wind picked up. It stoked the fire, drove it forwards, and blew the black smoke up into a huge cloud, a growing monstrosity alive with embers and flame. At one point a fireball burst from the belly of the cloud, soared in an arc as if launched from a catapult, landed at the foot of the hill before us, and the trees burst into flames. Smoke and ash blew in our faces, sometimes with a whiff of eucalyptus, sometimes with an ember as well.

As suddenly as the wind had picked up, it died down. The fire was no longer bent forwards, like someone running a race, but stood upright, as if awaiting instruction.

"You can go. If it becomes dangerous, I'll try to come. If I don't come, but the fire gets over the mountain, get in the boat and head out to sea. Don't wait for me. If the path to you gets cut off, I'll find another one."

# 19

Irene was lying as I had left her. I told her about the fire in the plain, about the wind, about Kari. She listened, but her eyelids were heavy. "Could you clean me up?" I fetched a new mattress and made up a bed, undressed Irene and washed her, then dressed her and moved her to the new bed. As I did so, she again put her arms trustingly around my neck, and it made me happy.

"If the fire comes over the mountain during the night, we'll get in the boat."

"I won't get in the boat."

That was so stupid that I had no idea how to respond. "Do you want to die in the fire? You aren't going to die when you want, you are going to die when it's your time."

"If the house burns down, it's my time. I won't burn, the smoke will suffocate me. It's an easy death." She said it mournfully and stubbornly, like a child clinging white-knuckled to the railing. "I don't want to go to Rock Harbour and to Sydney and to hospital. I don't want to die in a white room. I want to die here."

I leant over her and took her in my arms. "I won't let you die in a white room. You'll die here. When it's time. We'll get in the boat when the fire comes, and when it's gone, we'll move back into the old house and we'll have some more time together. We wasted so many days, we can't lose any more."

"Promise me that I'll die here? Whatever happens?"

I promised, and she let go of the balcony railing and fell asleep in my arms. Black smoke drifted over the mountains and rolled over the cove. Everything went dark, although I could still make out the dull white disc of the sun behind the smoke. Then I saw fire coming over the mountaintop. I lifted Irene up, carried her to the boat, soaked the towels and sheets in the old house and plastered them on the wood. A powerful wind came down from the hills. It bent and buffeted the trees, made the upper house groan and tremble, and whipped up the sea so the waves slapped the jetty. The air tasted of smoke and salt.

The fire rushed down the mountain and up the tree trunks into the crowns. They lit up like torches before they fell, or they exploded, throwing burning bark in the air. I ran to the boat and started the engine. Even down in the cove the firestorm roared, whirling sparks and ash through the air. The upper house was in flames; for a moment the gold-red fire outlined the edges and corners of the house and glowed from the windows, before the piles supporting the house buckled. It collapsed in on itself with a huge crash. The fire leapt to the old house on the beach, hissed through the beams, popped the windows from their frames, and the roof and veranda caved in.

The entire cove was burning. I headed out to sea, away from the cove, away from the heat and the scraps of burning bark and the embers and ashes. I do not know how long the fire raged, an hour, maybe two. Then only the afterglow

215

remained, orange under a red moon. I was completely exhausted. I lay down next to Irene, who hadn't woken up during the fire, and didn't wake up now. She shifted towards me, and as I laid my arm around her she nestled herself into the curve. That was how I fell asleep.

# 20

When I woke up, the day was bright, the sun was high in the sky and the boat was bobbing at the mouth of the cove. I sat up. The branches on the mountain trees were charred black skeletons, sometimes with rust-red crowns, or they had turned into thick or thin black totem poles, or they lay in a mess of black trunks. The upper house was a heap of charcoal, the lower one was blackened stone walls and columns, into which the roof and the veranda had collapsed.

Irene was gone. At first I didn't take it in, because I couldn't imagine it, then because I didn't want to take it in. Next to me, the mattress was empty, Irene was not sitting in the prow either, she wasn't huddled behind the helm, she didn't answer when I called her, and she didn't wave from the water where she had gone for a swim. As if she would have been capable of swimming. I started the engine and guided the boat to the jetty, crossing a warm carpet of gray ash to reach the beach house. I called out into the house, along the beach and up the hills. As if, while I was sleeping, she had been able to pilot the boat to the jetty, moor, go onshore, then send me back out to sea on the boat.

I sat down between the fallen roof tiles on the bench where Irene had woken me and greeted me, and didn't know how to bear that she was gone. That I could not see her face, hear her voice, touch her, hold her hand in mine. That she had woken up in the morning and seen the ruined old house, and thought she would now be taken to Rock Harbour and to Sydney to die in a white room. That she hadn't trusted me. But what could I have done? How could I not have taken her to hospital? Could we have lived on the boat until she died?

She had woken up in the morning, had struggled to the side of the boat, and let herself fall. Had she kissed me, stroked my hair or said something? Could I have woken up? I understood that she did not want to die in a white room. But I would have stayed with her day and night, we would have been close, we would have loved one another.

There is always something better than death. Could Irene not have known that? There is always something better than death, somewhere, whether in a white room in a hospital in the Outback or in Sydney. It must have happened differently from the way I had imagined. She had felt nauseous, as she had so often these past few days, she wanted to vomit over the side of the boat, and she had lost her balance and fallen in the water, too weak to swim or cry for help.

Kari came, saw that Irene was not there, asked no questions, said nothing, squatted down on the beach and stared out to sea. Could I hear plaintive humming notes from where he was squatting, beyond my field of vision? I don't know how much time passed, how long I sat and he squatted. Occasionally the notes of grief came into my ear. At some point I stood up and looked in his direction, but he was gone.

I went to the boat, took the bed out and dragged it onto

the charred rubble of the old house. I searched the boat and between oars, fishing gear, canisters, tubes, brushes and rags I found a piece of rope that was long enough to tie the wheel tight and keep the boat on course. I left my clothes on the beach, went back to the boat, started the engine and stayed on board until I could be sure that it was headed straight towards the centre of the mouth to the cove. Then I jumped in the water and swam back.

At first I had wanted to sink the boat. Sink it at the spot where I had woken up that morning and where, I thought, Irene had fallen into the sea. The boat as coffin or tombstone or burial offering at a place where I could grieve and say farewell. But then it felt like sinking the boat would make Irene's death even harder.

So I sat on the bench and watched the boat go. It crossed the quiet waters of the cove, reached the open sea, danced in the wind and waves, but it stayed on course and kept heading out to sea. The sea was empty; no container ships, no yachts, nothing except Irene's boat, which grew smaller and smaller in the afternoon light. Then I didn't know if I still saw it, or was just imagining it. That tiny black dot on the horizon – was that Irene's boat?

# 21

I looked out at the empty ocean and counted the days I had spent with Irene. They totalled fourteen – it was Tuesday, and I had arrived on a Tuesday, and we had been together not just one week, but not three either. It came to me how proud my children were when they learned to count to ten, or to a hundred, but they were in awe once they realized that numbers have no end, and thus discovered infinity.

I would look for Irene's daughter. I didn't know how to ensure that she got what was left of Irene's mother's estate. Irene must have been in contact with a bank or an attorney in Germany. How would I find them? How would I alert them to Irene's last wish? I wanted to ponder the problem, but I couldn't. I also couldn't fathom how I might approach my children. With a business proposition, by offering to set up a firm with them, as Irene had suggested? By slowly showing more interest in them and their children, so that we slowly grew closer? By telling them what had happened to me?

Although my thinking led me nowhere, I did not switch it off. But the knowledge of Irene's death again and again burst like a flood through the dam of thoughts I was attempting to erect. How could I live without her? How could I live without her? How, without her, could I live out what I had learned from her?

I ate some apples I had saved from the fire. I felt certain that the boat from Rock Harbour would soon come to check up on us. I would not perish here. But I couldn't escape the feeling that I had already perished. I didn't want my old life; I had looked forward to a new one – as if the new one could have been with her. I hadn't taken in that she was going to die.

Evening came, and night fell. I made a bed for myself in the ruins of the old house and while I was making it I found a couple of coins and my house keys and the keys to my rental car. My documents, my credit cards, my money – they had all burned in the fire, and I did not care. I lay there and again heard the waves washing ashore, the rush as they came in, the rustle back through the pebbles. I had never slept so close to the beach, and heard the rush and rustle so clearly. Smoke still hung in the air, and again and again the wind rose up and brought the scent of burned wood, sometimes with a note of eucalyptus, or dusted me with ash. I woke up at first light, watched the sun rise red from the sea, turn orange, then yellow as it set out across the sky.

I went up the hillside, poked around in the charred remains of the house, kicked the burned-out shell of the Jeep, stood before the dead black tree trunks. Then I noticed that between them there was life, here a couple of green blades of grass, there a couple of green branches. Disaster had come crashing down on the forest in such a frenzy, and rushed through it with such wild speed, that it hadn't been able to destroy everything small, only what was big. I climbed up to the top of the mountain. The hills ahead of me, the plain, the mountains in the distance — it all looked black. But up close there were traces of green everywhere. Traffic flowed along the motorway.

Then a boat steered into the cove, and I ran down the mountain. It was not Mark, but his father.

"You alone?"

"Irene is dead."

He nodded, as if he had expected it. "How did it happen?"

"She was very ill and weak, and she often felt nauseous. When the fire got here, I carried her to the boat and we sailed out into the cove. I think she must have felt sick during the night, and vomited over the side of the boat, and fell into the water. I have no other way to explain it. I was asleep, and in the morning she was gone."

"You should tell that to the Sheriff. She wasn't here legally, but everyone knew that she was here, and there might be questions." He looked around, looked at me and smiled. "You don't have any luggage?"

I smiled back. "No."

"Let's go."

# 22

My rental car was where I had left it in Rock Harbour, my cell phone still in the glove compartment. There were dozens of messages. I listened to the newest ones, a question from a colleague from my firm, a message from my cleaning lady, who was keeping an eye on my house in my absence, a reminder from the head of my travel agency that I urgently needed to postpone my flight again. I deleted those messages. I deleted all the others as well.

I spoke to the Sheriff, who made a note of Irene's death and took down my name and address. He had not known Irene, but he had known about her and done nothing. He had said to himself that time would take care of things.

I called the Australian colleague with whom I had prepared the merger. He was happy to lend me money and had the real-estate agency in Rock Harbour advance me some cash immediately. The German consulate in Sydney promised me new papers. The head of my travel agency had already postponed my flight, and postponed it again to two days later.

I spent the night in the same hotel by the sea that I had slept in on my journey out, sat on the terrace again, and watched the night fall. With the view of a marina and the noise of a busy restaurant, it wasn't what it had been in

Irene's cove. That made me sad, and because I was afraid I might cry I went to my room. But I didn't cry, not this time, nor any of the many other times I felt a lump in my throat.

I stopped in the same hotel in Sydney I had stayed in before Rock Harbour, and once again I was given a room with a view over the Opera House, the bay, and at the end of the bay, the green strip of land that separated it from the ocean. My Australian colleague invited me to dinner and I made the mistake of telling him about Irene. He winked at me conspiratorially and waxed lyrical about the young secretary he'd been having a fling with these past two weeks. The German consul greeted me personally, and kindly asked how I had managed to get myself into and out of a wildfire, and gave me temporary papers.

The question of whether I should go to see the painting spun round and round in my head. Sometimes I lost myself in a dream in which everything began again, and I went to the Art Gallery and saw the painting and thought that I had stumbled upon the past, whereas in fact I had come across the future. I longed to see Irene again, and I didn't care that I might cry. But I was afraid of the sadness that was sometimes unbearable, and I longed for the old Irene who had come down the stairs to me, not the young Irene, so I decided not to go. But I went anyway; the painting was gone, and I was told it was on its way to New York.

I didn't tell anyone I was coming back. No car to pick me up, no chauffeur to recount what had happened in Frankfurt, no flowers would be on my desk. The taxi dropped me off. I unlocked the door and walked through my house like a stranger. Yes, that was the furniture my wife and I had bought, the pictures we'd found at the Frankfurt art dealer we befriended, the three wooden saints we had discovered in Buenos Aires. Those were the rooms where the children still slept when they came to visit, although they had removed everything of importance to them. That was our – my – bedroom; I had cleared my wife's clothes out of the closet, but had changed nothing else. My cleaning lady had laid my dressing gown on the bed. After returning from a trip and unpacking and showering, I liked to wear it to read the mail that had piled up in my absence. There was a lot of it.

I would wait until tomorrow to go to the firm. Today I would go to the cemetery and talk to my wife. I wanted to ask her forgiveness. I also wanted to say goodbye and explain to her why I could no longer live in our house and with our things. I wanted to tell her about Irene. I would call my children. I would prepare myself for the meeting with Karchinger and the other partners. I would have no answer to many of their questions. But what did that matter.

## AUTHOR'S NOTE

The painting of Irene on the staircase may remind some readers of Gerhard Richter's *Ema* (*Nude on a Staircase*). In fact, a postcard of Richter's painting has stood on my desk for years, in rotation with other postcards and photographs. Nevertheless, Irene's painter, Karl Schwind, has nothing to do with Gerhard Richter, and is purely fictional.

*blog and newsletter*

For literary discussion, author insight,
book news, exclusive content,
recipes and giveaways, visit the
Weidenfeld & Nicolson blog and
sign up for the newsletter at:

# www.wnblog.co.uk

For breaking news, reviews and exclusive competitions
Follow us 🐦 @wnbooks
Find us 📘 facebook.com/WeidenfeldandNicolson